Roy Jacobsen

Roy Jacobsen (1954–) is one of the most celebrated and influential contemporary writers in Norway, with his ten novels, four collections of short stories, a biography and a children's book. Among other awards, Roy Jacobsen has won the Bookseller's Prize, the Critic's Prize and in 2006, the Gyldendal Prize for *The Burnt-Out Town of Miracles*.

D0594684

The Burnt-Out Town
of Miracles

ROY JACOBSEN

Translated by
Don Bartlett and Don Shaw

JOHN MURRAY

First published in Great Britain in 2007 by John Murray (Publishers)
An Hachette Livre UK company

First published in Norway in 2005 by J.W. Cappelens Forlag AS

First published in paperback in 2008

3

A CIP catalogue record for this title is available from the British Library

ISBN 978-0-7195-2112-6

Typeset in Monotype Perpetua by Servis Filmsetting Ltd, Manchester

Printed and bound by Clays Ltd

John Murray policy is to use papers that are natural, renewable and recyclable products and
made from wood grown in sustainable forests. The logging and manufacturing processes are
expected to conform to the environmental regulations of the country of origin.

John Murray (Publishers)
338 Euston Road
London NW1 3BH

www.johnmurray.co.uk

To my children — Maria and Daniel

I

Suomussalmi was set ablaze on 7 December, after all four thousand inhabitants had been evacuated, except for me, I was born here, had lived here all my life and couldn't imagine living anywhere else – so when I became aware of a figure in a white uniform standing in front of me, reading from a piece of paper and telling me I had to get out, I dug my heels into the snow and refused to budge. I suppose it is like that all over the world, there is always one, at least one, who doesn't follow the crowd, he doesn't even need to know why, and here in Suomussalmi it was me.

Strangely enough, standing there, a lonely pillar of salt, watching the vast sea of flames in the freezing forests was both terrible and exhilarating, because it had been a fine town, my town, the only one I knew that was more than a collection of roofs and walls. And now there were only a few houses left; I could not count more than twenty when it was all over.

Even Antti, the grocer, had said to me before he left, you can't stay here, Timo, the Russians will be here at any time, and they will kill you.

'They don't kill idiots,' I had answered. 'I know the Russians.'

'Come on, Timo, they kill everyone, whether they know them or not. This is war.'

Then I had no choice but to repeat what I had said, no one would touch me, but it seemed unnecessary, instead I looked at Antti the way I usually did when words were unnecessary – Antti, the man I have worked for since my parents died and who has never called me any names, even though maybe sometimes he hasn't been happy with either my behaviour or my work.

'The logs should be shorter,' he would say.

'You said they should be half a metre long,' I would reply, sometimes getting out my metre rule and slapping it against my palm as a kind of threat to prove the truth unless he retracted his words.

'The church hasn't got a tunnel stove,' he might go on, 'and now the priest won't buy the wood.'

'Sell it to Marja, then.'

2

'Her café's deserted these days.'

'What about if I chop the logs in half, so they're twenty-five centimetres. Then you can sell them to Mäkinen. His school has got small stoves, hasn't it?'

'That's double the work,' Antti would say, 'and you earn almost nothing as it is.'

But *that* is beside the point. Because your personal circumstances are usually your own business, most people would agree, so it's strange that it has to be repeated so often; in any case, I didn't need money, I had the farm and land and the forest, I could fish and hunt, I got free milk and flour and also a few tins of food from Antti, or he deducted the cost from the pay I got for the wood. It didn't make any difference, as long as he set the price for both milk and wood, it would stay low, as he was not only tight-fisted, but also felt sorry for me – most people in the district feel sorry for me unless my appearance annoys them or they make fun of me for some other reason. But it didn't bother me because the same people who feel sorry for me one minute often make fun of me the next, as if their compassion wears them down; one day they call me an idiot and the next they give me milk or pork, I don't often get both at the same time, I'm the kind of person who gets bits at a time, which means I've had to learn to save the little I have, even though it might be worth nothing in other people's eyes.

*

Now I was helping Antti and his two young sons to pack. There was no end to what he felt they had to take with them.

'Aren't you planning to come back?' I asked, carrying out the spinning wheel and the massive sewing machine he hadn't found any use for since Anna, his wife, died.

'Yes,' he answered, 'but the house will be burned down, and I don't want to see that. Get a move on.'

'Aren't you going to build a new house when you get back?'

'Yes, and it's going to be built right here. This land's not going anywhere.'

'I'll look after it.'

But Antti didn't smile that day. He said it was the saddest he had experienced in all his forty-five years, perhaps with the exception of the time Anna died – that happened almost a year ago to the day.

We filled both the large sled and the two small ones with furniture and bedlinen and clothes and cutlery, as well as Anna's things, and we emptied the shop of tins and dried food, the rest we destroyed. The stoves were all that remained in the unfamiliar, gaping rooms. It had turned into a house with echoes and grey dustballs sweeping along the skirting boards like terrified rats.

'Can I live here?' I asked, nodding towards the back room where I had a bed and also kept a few of my things.

4

'It'll be *burnt down*!' Antti shouted. 'Can't you get that into your thick skull!'

'If I stay here perhaps I'll be able to save it,' I said. 'Then you don't have to build a new one when you get back.'

Antti looked as if he felt sorry for me and despised me at the same time. But then he put a hand on my shoulder and sadly looked away, that was one of his habits, to look away when he knew that just the sight of me could strain our fragile friendship.

'You'll be shot,' he said. 'The order's from Mannerheim himself.'

'That's my business,' I said.

And that was that, inasmuch as we had both got what we wanted, as we usually do, without either of us deriving any satisfaction from it.

We agreed that Antti should also take Kävi, my horse. Then, with a groan, he manoeuvred his huge body into the first sled and took the reins of the horse behind, which was pulling the sled in which Harri, his oldest son, was sitting, holding the reins of the horse harnessed to the last sled, where Jussi was sitting, and bringing up the rear was Kävi, trotting along as free as the wind, which made them look like a little train, a locomotive with two small carriages as they slid off on creaking runners towards Hulkonniemi bridge, and not one of them looked back, as far as I could see, because I stood on the steps and waved until they had disappeared, together with hundreds of other sleds and cars and animals, and some tractors too, every living thing left Suomussalmi on this, the darkest day in Antti's life, 7 December 1939.

No town has ever been so quiet. No lights anywhere, no steps to be heard on the dry, powdery snow, no voices, no cows lowing, no dogs barking, no horses or cattle stamping and snorting in their stalls, the sounds of the town were gone, and most of all – no smoke from the chimneys; what had been a town of four thousand inhabitants and as many animals, if not more, had been transformed in the course of a few hours into a hotchpotch of empty wooden shells, holding their breath in the freezing winter that had wrought havoc in these forests since the time before animals and humans had even thought of being created.

I left the shop and roamed the sudden emptiness, as if to touch and feel it. But then I noticed that many of the doors were unlocked, indeed open, and that a few people had gathered small piles of straw and wood so that it would be easier for the soldiers to set fire to their houses, and I recognised a lot of the wood, it was mine, the way it had been cut and split, I almost have my own trademark when it comes to wood. Some people had even carried the wood indoors, scattered it with straw and newspaper over the floors, and stacked it on staircases and in cupboards. And it was obvious that not everyone had taken as many of their belongings as Antti had done. In one house only the bedroom furniture had gone, in another the kitchen had apparently been the most valued possession, in a third it looked as if thieves had been at work, or a kind of panic had set in — an unholy mess, as if they had deliberately wrecked the furniture and everything else.

But in a cottage belonging to old Luukas and his wife, whom we called Aunt Roosa, nothing appeared to have been touched — quite the contrary, every room smelled clean, the beds were carefully made, and it was as tidy as if they had prepared the house for Christmas. On the walls hung photographs of their three sons and the old couple's family in Raatevaara, the small town close to the border where it was said the Russians broke through less than a week ago, the troops that were now on their way to Suomussalmi.

I had often delivered wood to Luukas and Roosa, and the old man had taken a photo of me once too, standing next to Kävi and the wood-cart, like some kind of chieftain. But as a rule only photographs of the family are put on walls, so I was safely tucked away in a drawer somewhere. But I didn't touch anything, just walked around and gazed at this strange, newly cleaned scene of orderliness — all anyone could need, memories to boot, but it was all dead, as dead as snow.

*

But this made me determined to save the house, as well as Antti's, so I found a hayfork and went to work on the pile of straw Luukas had left outside the door, raked it into the barn and down to the dung cellar. There I found half a slaughtered pig, which the old couple must have forgotten, or else they had intended it to go up in smoke with the barn.

Without a second thought – it was the obvious thing to do – I started to cut up the half-frozen pig, wrapped the pieces of meat in a tarpaulin and hung them in a spruce tree some way into the forest, where they would keep in the sub-zero temperatures for weeks and months on end, if left in peace by the animals. And it was while I stood wondering whether I should set a marten trap that I heard the war for the first time, a distant drone of engines slowly approaching through the windless winter, from the same direction in which the evacuees had disappeared, then the sound of firing in the far distance, from the east, the boom of artillery.

I walked back through the dark streets and came to Antti's shop as the first military vehicles rolled over the bridge, and a jeep stopped right in front of me – while the others continued into town, full of white-uniformed soldiers, who jumped out and forced their way into the defenceless houses, carrying straw, firewood and cans of kerosene.

A man in his thirties got out of the jeep and looked me up and down with disbelief, a living human being in a town that was about to be annihilated.

'What are you doing here?' he asked.

'I live here,' I said.

'This town has to be evacuated,' he said. 'The Russians will be here in . . . maybe even tomorrow.'

'That doesn't bother me.'

Again, he gave the impression of being completely bemused by the man standing before him. His driver jumped out and they started to talk in low voices, but there has never been anything wrong with my hearing, and the man who had spoken to me, and who was obviously an officer, returned and asked if I was the village idiot. He said it without the slightest hint of all the nasty sneers that existed, as if he was asking a completely normal question, about, say, how old I was, so I answered, quite simply, yes, I suppose I was, and that I was staying here even if he threatened to shoot me, for I would never leave Suomussalmi, there are more important things in life than just a miserable human life.

That certainly made him smile, albeit reluctantly.

'Have you got a gun?' he asked after a while, chewing on the slivers of ice that dangled from his ragged moustache.

I went into the back room, to Antti's stores where I had also stacked my tools and the food I had, came out again and showed him the rifle.

'A Moisin,' he said thoughtfully, stroking the old gem with his bare hands, and I could sense that he was impressed at how well kept it was. 'An army rifle?'

'Yes. My father's.'

'Have you got ammunition, too?'

I gave him the ammunition, too. He put it and the rifle in the car, and half turned to me again, still apparently pondering the matter that had caused him so much trouble he was unable to get on with what he was doing.

Through the windows of the houses closest to us the flames could be seen rising, and men ran back and forth, shouting, between the cars and the buildings. As the first windowpanes exploded, the houses on either side of Antti's cottage were fully ablaze, after what sounded like a double explosion. We had to retreat from the intense heat. The officer signalled to the driver to move the car to a safe distance and he himself walked slowly behind while I remained where I was, the heat on my back like a searing sun.

After just a few steps he stopped and walked back, took me down the street towards the bridge, pulled out a tobacco pouch and asked if I wanted a cigarette.

I said no.

'We have to burn down that one, too,' he said with a nod towards Antti's shop as two white columns of smoke emerged from his quivering nostrils.

'*I* can do that,' I offered. And again this thoughtful expression came over his face and led nowhere. 'I'm not scared,' I added. 'Not of anything.'

Now the heat had become so intense that we could no longer remain even in the street. I had seen fires before, but that was from a distance, and a single house, and what I was now unable to grasp was not so much this unbearable heat, but the sounds, one explosion after another, like a massive volcanic eruption, and where did the terrible wind come from? There was a full-blown storm raging through the windless inferno.

'A war without fires is like a sausage without mustard,' the officer screamed in my ear. 'Come on.'

He set off towards the bridge. And all I could do was run after him, I did catch him up too, and ran at his side for some time. It was no problem keeping up, although it is difficult to say whether he was making an effort to leave me behind, he ran at quite a relaxed pace, yet it still seemed to annoy him that I could keep up so easily, all the way down to the bridge where the vehicles had gathered to await new orders – Suomussalmi is built on a headland jutting into Lake Kiantajärvi, which stretches for many miles and winds its way around the town like a rough-edged serpent, and now I could see that the houses on the opposite headland were on fire as well, but there were far fewer of them, so I presumed the regiment would be able to get through unscathed, unless, that is, they had planned to cross the ice to the southern side of the lake, which *I* would have done, had I been in command of these troops and had plans to recapture a town which, for tactical reasons, I had originally reduced to ashes.

But I didn't say that, and now the officer stared at me again with his winter-weary eyes before he finally seemed annoyed enough to make a decision.

'I can't let you keep the rifle,' he said. 'It would just make matters even worse . . . for you.'

I nodded.

'Look after it for me,' I said.

He mumbled a tetchy yes, absent-minded now, whereupon the tiny smile reappeared. And only after he had barked a number of orders at his soldiers and the cars had started to roll over the bridge did I realise that for the last time he was weighing up the chances of removing me by brute force, or possibly whether he could even be bothered to be concerned about me at all.

'You haven't slept for a long time,' I said.

He looked up in surprise.

'Not since last week, no, why?'

I stepped back a few paces.

'You won't get me out of here, no matter what,' I shouted. 'I'll just run into the flames, finish it all.'

Eventually he seemed to understand that I meant what I said. Then his car pulled up, he opened the door, said something to the driver, turned to me, holding a white anorak, and mumbled something about it protecting me against the cold — at least against being spotted if I did decide to escape. But I didn't move a muscle.

'Are the Russians white or black?' I asked.

He began to laugh, slung the anorak back in the car and shouted:

'Black! As black as the devil himself!'

Then he slurred a 'Good luck', so low that I couldn't hear it, either that or he unleashed a stream of abuse, I preferred to think he had wished me luck before he got in, and the car drove off behind the others, over the bridge towards Hulkonniemi, westwards, away from the advancing Russians.

I would meet this officer again; his name was Olli, and at this stage he had the rank of lieutenant, the same as my father had. When the war was over, Olli would *still* have the rank of lieutenant, as opposed to my father, who rose to become a captain in the course of *his* war.

2

I ran back to the town and saw that Antti's house was not yet ablaze, at least it wasn't burning the way it was meant to, the kitchen was only smouldering, and the smoke, like thick curdled milk, pressed against the windows in the sitting room and bedrooms. But because of the flames from the neighbour's house it was impossible to approach from the front, so I ran around and was about to kick in the back door, the entrance I used when Antti didn't want to see me, when it occurred to me that this was probably all it needed, a sudden draught, so instead I set about cramming snow into gaps and cellar windows to seal the house even more effectively.

Yet another explosion ripped through what was already a deafening roar – it was the bridge going up – and in the unreal flashes of light over by Hulkonniemi I could see the ice in the sound breaking up, the lake looking like a river in the spring thaw. In the background, in the gradually lightening wall of shadow from the forest, I spotted many tiny water-like ripples which combined to form a grey river running gently across the ice towards the ferry berth on Lake Haukiperä, the route I would have taken with my soldiers if I had been Olli or his commanding officer.

But I don't know whether it had a calming effect on me, you don't think clearly at moments like these, I really wasn't thinking at all, I only did what I was doing, stuffing snow into gaps and crevices as I watched the last route to the west go up in flames.

Now the smoke in Antti's house looked like a dense wall behind the rime-frosted windows, but it was still grey, fortunately, not yellow, not red, and I realised that it would survive, both the living area and the shop.

I walked around the shop and into the storeroom, found my tools and my food-bag and took refuge in the forest – and I stood there for hours watching everything the people of Suomussalmi had created and accumulated over the years going up in black smoke, set alight by the very same people or their leaders, and, oddly enough, what hit me hardest was the sight of the burning school, which I had often dreamed of setting fire to myself when I was a pupil there; there went my childhood, my memories and friends, good and bad, and the little church, which seemed to burn better than anything else, whatever the reason for that might be, and which only now I realised was possibly the most beautiful building in the whole town, that was where I was christened and confirmed and where I had also assumed I would be buried, like my parents – at first the sea of flames looked like a gigantic, ruptured star, its untamed arms reaching out to cover the whole town, then a hissing snake, then a sack of storm clouds, billowing back and forth in this insane windless storm, building up to a climax and subsiding again in the course of moments, just like when a mountain-side collapses, I thought, that was what it was, a landslide.

I had to stay in the forest until late into the night. The snow on the trees was melting, drops of water fell through the biting frost, becoming hail and white pebbles before hitting the soot-blackened soil with the sound of a horse being branded. The foundation walls were smouldering, bare earth had appeared everywhere, covered in soot and mud, looking like festering sores, gangrene, before the frost froze them again and transformed house-less streets and alleys into forlorn, grey concrete. But when the morning came, in so far as morning can come after a night like this, the atmosphere was, oddly enough, not as unreal as when everything was quiet and the houses still stood quaking like defenceless children. This is how a burnt-out town *should* look, like a festering crater in white skin, this is what you expect of a burnt-out town, it is horrible, it is inconceivable, and yet it is still exactly as it should be.

But I did discover around twenty buildings were still standing, large and small, burned and half burned, and among them not only Antti's shop, but also Luukas and Aunt Roosa's cottage, which I had locked as a precaution. Only the porch and part of the eaves had been destroyed by the fire, so I could go straight through the green kitchen door and see the photographs of the sons and the relatives from Raatevaara still hanging on the wall, and I knew immediately that I was going to live *here*, and not in Antti's empty, smoke-damaged shop, here in Roosa and Luukas's house I had everything, chairs and tables and beds, plates and cutlery, everything except for food, but I had the pig in the tree and the little I had grabbed when we were loading Antti's sleds.

In the pantry I also found a jar of lard, a bucket of frozen milk and a sack of coarse salt. The barn had been burned, but not to the ground. I started to pull down the blackened remains and chop them into firewood. The walls had been made of timber, dry spruce, and by evening I had a sizeable pile of wood that would last at least three to four weeks.

I walked back to the forest, fetched the pig, salted half of the meat and hung the rest in the freezing-cold pantry.

Then I made myself a meal as though I lived there, and ate, and thought that if only I'd had some coffee I would almost have been comfortable. And with that thought in my mind, I fell asleep – with my head between the scraps left on the table, dreaming that I was standing before a locked door, unable to find my name – I wouldn't be let in unless I found my name, but where was it? I rubbed my eyes until my eyesight went, still without having found a name – I didn't wake until I had totally given up, and by then I was exhausted.

In a mirror on the wall above the slop sink I saw that my eyes were as red as crushed lingonberries, brimful of smoke and water, my eyebrows and hair were singed, my cheeks flaming red, and the skin on my nose as thin as flies' wings. But there was no option but to get dressed and go out to have a closer look at the town, there was no way round it, and I have often been asked since whether I felt any regret at having stayed behind, but the answer is always no, not even at that moment, and I never will.

It had been snowing during the however many hours I had slept, and the silence was deeper than I have ever known, not even gunfire could be heard in the forests, only a winter at its deadest, both in heaven and on earth.

There wasn't much to be found in the smouldering ruins, apart from swirling soot and some blue scrap metal that I poked out with an iron bar and began to scrape together as it cooled down in the snow, once again without asking myself why – it is as if you see a mess and you have to try to tidy up, especially things you like, and I have always had a liking for tools and things; I found handle-less spades and forks, crowbars, saw-blades, bits of chain, harnesses and tools with handles and tools minus the leather and the grip, all amputated limbs which I spent the brunt of the day collecting and putting in a pile outside Luukas and Roosa's house. It started out as a mechanical exercise, but bit by bit it became more like a game, and I thought it wouldn't be too hard to repair everything, to forge new shafts and handles for all this equipment that had once been so valuable and essential for this town in order for it to be able to remain what it was – screwdrivers, hammer and sledgehammer heads, braces, wood chisels, cant hooks, wedges, broad axes, horseshoes, pram frames, water pumps, ladder fittings, paraffin lamps, window hasps and bicycle wheels . . . Several of the objects could barely be identified, the innards of an old clock, the charred remains of boot cleats, a dog chain, what had once been a jewellery box, berry-pickers, door handles, shelf brackets, a handful of pen nibs – I found those in the ruins of the school – a globe stand, twisted skeletons in a heap with blinds and bundles of electric cables resembling fossilised insects.

In the cellar under the log-floaters' cabin, which hadn't been fire damaged though the roof and walls had been ripped off when the bridge exploded, I also found an almost half-full two-kilo can of coffee, and in the neighbouring house hidden beneath the smouldering trapdoor to the cellar were a sack of scorched-brown flour and a basket of black, hard-boiled eggs; in another cellar I found four jars of rhubarb jam, boiled for a second time, plus a jug of warm vodka, five bulging unlabelled cans of food and several kilos of sooty oats.

Encouraged by all this, I began to search the remaining houses, but, inside, they were as eerie as the streets had been before the fire. I wandered among naked people no longer breathing, I touched almost nothing, I looked, and time after time had to nod with disappointment at finding the pantries empty.

But then I made two discoveries: first of all, the town had not been depleted of all living things, the cats were still there, some of them I saw with my own eyes, I saw only the tracks of others, and more and more paw-prints appeared, running criss-cross over the snow that lay like a carpet of sparkling white flour all over the black.

Then I came across a letter on the kitchen table in the house behind the school belonging to an old woman we called Babushka, although she was just as Finnish as the rest of us, because she had been as bent and grey as timber for as long as anyone could remember. She had left her home behind in the same clean and tidy condition that Luukas and

Roosa had. And I felt this had the makings of a little mystery, so I opened the letter and read it.

The old woman's handwriting was difficult to read, but I am a good reader, and on the paper she had first drawn some shaky lines with a ruler, and had then written with an equally shaky pencil that the soldiers could burn everything to the ground without feeling any shame, the only reason she had washed and cleaned her house was so that the gift she gave to Finland would be worthy.

But the house was also unharmed.

Then I discovered that the letter had been resealed, it had been torn open by impatient, dirty fingers and had presumably been read before I arrived; on the floor of the otherwise tidy kitchen lay a pile of straw and logs; the rag rug stank of paraffin and a canister had been flung into a corner by the sink. I looked for some matches or other signs of a failed attempt to set the house on fire, but found none.

After I had sat for a while and read the letter one more time, or rather looked at it, the way you can sit and stare at letters without really reading them as your mind struggles with things you can't quite comprehend, I began to realise that the soldier who had been going to light the fire had read the letter and had then been unable to execute the order, to burn this gift to Finland.

I wondered whether that meant we would lose this war and perish, as a nation. But then I reasoned that a country with such mothers and soldiers *cannot* lose, no matter what happens, these people survive when others don't; so it was a great joy to discover that four more of the other houses were so clean and tidy that the sun shone brightly in each of the abandoned rooms. In the one nearest to Luukas's I found a wall clock which I decided to borrow, or protect, it wasn't clear which, but I took it with me at any event, a wall clock with all the cogwheels intact, the clock face, the key and the hands, and also the sound, like the heartbeat of a creature which has to be mankind's last friend.

I went back and stoked up the big stove in Roosa's kitchen, hammered in a blue nail with one of the hammer heads and hung the clock on the wall between the photographs of the relatives from Raatevaara, and then I began to bake bread and roast coffee beans, and I ate more slowly and better than I had for a long time – for dessert I had lukewarm stewed rhubarb with a splash of milk. When I had finished, it was evening.

There were lamps and paraffin in the house, and candles, but I decided to sit and wait until the darkness, in its own way, had extinguished this, the strangest day of my life, this day that because of the silence, the cat's paw marks and the clean houses had transformed or turned upside down the machinery inside me which thinks even when I don't, or perhaps rather, a day that took me back to the person I was before all this happened. At such moments it is difficult to know whether you are changing or just learning to understand yourself.

When it was completely dark, I went outside to listen — and heard nothing. Not a single sound. I thought this strange, but then it would have been even stranger if I had heard something. This war that surrounded me on all sides and yet wasn't there, it was like tomorrow, it doesn't come until it comes.

I went back in, locked the door and went upstairs to bed in the room I knew had belonged to Luukas and Roosa's youngest son, Markku, who was now a soldier on the Karelian isthmus, where the war was real and not just a paralysis of all living things, where the soldiers were already dying like flies, both Russians and Finns. With my hands I could feel that the skin on my face was no longer burning, it was just rough and grainy and numb, as it should be when you have lived through something terrible, but you have come to terms with it.

3

My thoughts are never as lofty as when I slowly wake up in a bed I don't need to get out of. Then I think of an ocean of trees, of the tree trunks it takes a human being — or a wild storm — to upend, all pointing in the same direction, as if obeying an order, like soldiers, or fence posts, and the wind, which is the voice of the forest, along with the cracking of frozen branches and birdsong, the buzzing of insects and rain, while the snow doesn't say much, but it is the sound of chains I hear as again I stand before the huge door and cannot find my name — champing iron belts and the roar of engines, running boots and shouts as the house and bed shake and are tossed around like a coffee cup in an empty, runaway hay-wagon.

Still I take my time, not that I think about it, I just remember that I take my time, before getting out of bed and stepping out of sleep and dressing for another day and going slowly downstairs to the kitchen, where a stranger swivels round when he hears me and points a rifle at my chest, the panic shining out of his filthy, ungroomed face — the next moment he starts screaming.

I know he is screaming orders, and that they are directed at me, but they are given in a language I only know a few words of, so I raise my arms and try to smile reassuringly while I slowly back into the street, almost tumble over the pile of scrap iron now covered with rime frost and snow, and I see the razed town is again full of people, swarms of men, running, walking, driving, riding, strangers, figures dressed in black and their machines which have shattered the silence and filled everything with smells and sounds that have never been here before, thousands of alien figures who all have something unsteady and strange about them, as if they have emerged from the ground and cannot cope with daylight.

They stream towards me from all sides and stare at me with unseeing eyes. And since no one appears to want to make a decision — they only brandish their rifles and all shout at once as if furiously disagreeing — I walk calmly on in front of the impatient gun barrel, still with my hands above my head, I run the gauntlet of white faces, blue lips and incomprehensible jeers, towards a group of tanks that has taken up position in the square in front of the burnt-out school, where I am met by a man I know is an officer.

He stands with both palms raised as if in a Red Indian greeting, but I know he will stop me, so I stop, at a respectful distance, and I hear him shout something over his shoulder to a fair-haired man coming out of the enormous tent, the only man in the gathering not wearing a helmet but a fur hat with the earflaps turned up. He looks like a Finn and addresses me in my own language, admittedly broken Finnish, and only a curt greeting at first, but I return it.

There is a silence before he starts to translate for me what the officer says, or barks, for the interpreter has a friendlier or softer tone than his superior, and I have a vague feeling that I have seen him before, the interpreter, that is, perhaps it is because of his language, which gets better and better as the interrogation goes on, not that it gets us anywhere as all I can do is repeat over and over again that I am the only remaining person in town, and that I refused to be evacuated because I live here and will never go anywhere else, no matter what happens. And as I say this — a word-for-word repetition of what I said to Antti and Olli — I can feel that the words sound more right and more real, almost as though they were planned, which of course they are not, it is total madness what I am saying, everyone knows that, but it cannot be any other way, because it is true.

But the officer only becomes angrier and angrier at all these answers of mine that don't change, and the interpreter asks why, why . . . until I say:

'I'm the logger here. I deliver wood to all the houses and keep everyone warm.'

Now there is real silence. The confused officer develops something like tiny tics – control or compromise? – in his lean face before suddenly bursting into raucous laughter, which the soldiers hesitantly join in, one after the other, until soon close on a hundred alien men are standing on the pitch-black ice laughing as though they had never heard anything funnier.

But laughter is certainly better than loaded guns, and there aren't any of them pointing in my direction any longer, so I venture to lower my arms, but remain where I am, as a sign that I have understood that it's the officer, not me, who decides whether I should move or not, and this seems to give him further reassurance.

He comes closer and inspects me, as if I might have been pretending to be who I am, while I anxiously return his gaze. He is a man of at least forty, broad shouldered and erect with a prominent nose and narrow, bitter lips that he constantly sinks his teeth into, and his eyes are as sleep-deprived and weary as Olli's, his face drawn and lean with weeks-old stubble growing in irregular clumps on surprisingly white skin.

'Are you cold?' I ask, almost believing that I have finally found what is wrong with them, these lame, shuffling movements, they are worn out, all of them, on the verge of collapse.

'Is that a question?' the interpreter asks with flat intonation, looking away.

'Yes,' I say. 'He looks frozen, and as though he has been for a long time.'

Now this question can be interpreted as having something to do with my wood, which I was just talking about, with heating and freezing temperatures, and not with the war. And as far as I can judge, the interpreter decides to translate it in that way. But then something happens between these two men that I don't quite catch, as the officer suddenly seems to be more irritated with the interpreter than with me, and the interpreter seems to be defending himself.

'Did you translate what I said?' I break in.

'Shut up,' he barks over his shoulder, and responds to further accusations before turning back to me.

'He doesn't believe you asked if he was cold.'

'Repeat it, and tell him I want to show him something.'

The interpreter thinks about this, says a few dispassionate Russian words and just stands there staring resolutely at the tips of his boots. The officer looks from him to me and mumbles something out of the corner of his mouth. The interpreter nods soberly, and turns to face me once more.

'Are you really Finnish?'

'Of course.'

'Papers?'

'At home, on the farm, twenty kilometres north of here, in Lonkkaniemi.'

He translates, receives a curt nod and a couple of grunted words.

'What do you want to show us?'

I point to Luukas and Roosa's house and make a gesture with my hand intended to show that I am an obedient servant welcoming his masters. The officer considers for a second, then motions that he will follow, at a distance. And we walk in file to the house, where I open the door and hold it open, to little purpose, as the officer refuses to go in before his soldiers have searched the building, from cellar to loft, for booby-traps and mines, I suppose. And in the meantime I show him the pile of wood I have made, the remnants of Luukas's barn wall. But he just gives a stiff nod, starts to kick at the pile of scrap metal and, through the translator, asks what it is. Tools and equipment that I plan to repair some time, I tell him, a plan which seems to confirm the perception of me that is beginning to form in his mind.

The officer receives an all-clear from his soldiers, shrugs and along with the interpreter and two privates, we walk into the kitchen. He sits down at Luukas and Roosa's table while I busy myself making coffee and slicing bread, and the soldiers take up their positions at the doors.

The officer says something, but the interpreter neither answers nor translates. The officer says something again, and it sounds like the same words.

'What's he saying?' I ask.

'He asked me not to translate.'

'But it was to me?'

The interpreter says something to the officer, who seems to be torn out of his reverie. He answers briefly, but without any reluctance.

'He says the town has been burnt down,' says the interpreter, making it sound like a question.

'So that you wouldn't find anything here,' I say. 'Neither food nor shelter.'

'He understands that, but he believes it could be a trap.'

In my mind's eye I see again the shadows running like a grey river over the ice on Lake Kiantajärvi as the town was burning.

'So why did you walk into it?'

Again, the interpreter looks as though he cannot believe what he is hearing, then suddenly he starts shouting, into the air, presumably frightened to vent his fury on anything in particular. But at this moment the soldier standing guard at the front door faints and comes to again as he hits the floor and leaps back into place, mumbling something that must have been an apology. I assume from their bloated faces that it is the sudden heat which is affecting them and hand the soldier a slice of bread. He casts a fleeting glance at the officer, who looks away, then grabs the bread and bolts it down like a starving dog. I give his comrade a slice as well, which he eats in the same way, while the officer waves his hand irritably and the interpreter again looks directly at me, now appearing to choose his words with care.

'What do *you* think?' he asks, again about this trap that they believe the Finns may have laid for them. And I know the question might be dangerous, but perhaps it could also be my salvation, if I answer in a way that will convince the officer I am not only stupid but also as harmless as he obviously hopes.

'I don't know,' I say, pouring coffee into Roosa's cups and pushing the best one towards the officer, who immediately clasps it in a stranglehold between his filthy fingerless gloves.

'But what do *you* think?' the interpreter barks again. Without allowing myself to lose my composure, I also give the two privates some coffee, which they slurp loudly, to the officer's obvious annoyance. Calmly, I say to the interpreter:

'Would you translate something you didn't think he would like to hear?'

'What?'

I repeat the question.

'Of course!'

'Then I'd like you to tell him I think you speak bad Finnish, especially when you're angry.'

I look down, but I can sense the interpreter blushing, probably tempted to fling the coffee in my face. Instead he reels off a few sentences in Russian, and the officer stares at him in surprise before bursting into raucous laughter once again.

'I don't understand everything you say,' I hasten to add. 'You must excuse me.'

The interpreter translates that as well, judging by the officer's reaction, because he says some very long sentences, during which his face relaxes more and more, as if some fears have finally turned out to be unfounded. When, at long last, the interpreter lets me take part in the conversation, he too has become calmer, but now there is greater menace and suspicion in his eyes. I don't like it.

'We don't have any transport for prisoners,' he says in his monotone. 'But you can join the supplies division, they need loggers.'

I nod. He says:

'And I hardly need to mention that you'll be shot if we have the slightest suspicion that . . .'

I send him a questioning look.

'Can you repeat that?'

He repeats it, now more irritated than suspicious.

'That suits me fine,' I say when I finally understand what he is driving at. 'I like cutting wood.'

We stare at each other for a long time until something changes, a sort of truce, I hope, at least he seems to have accepted that I am no danger.

I ask if they would like to know who owned the house they are sitting in, before it was given to Finland and the war.

'No,' says the interpreter.

I repeat the question.

'No,' he repeats. 'But we'd like to hear why it hasn't been burnt down, if that's not too much trouble?'

'Because I looked after it,' I answer, and go over to the wall behind one of the guards and take down a photograph of Luukas and Roosa and put it on the table in front of the officer, pointing to the old couple and saying their names. He glances at them absent-mindedly.

'They came from Raatevaara thirty years ago,' I say. 'Luukas settled here as a cobbler and craftsman, he built this house himself, they've got three sons who are all fighting in the war . . .'

But the interpreter does not translate, he seems drained, and the officer doesn't show the slightest sign of interest either, he just sits there staring at the photograph, as though it reminds him of something – there's something familiar about everything, and then he raises his eyes and stares straight at me. I stare back. He lifts his cup as if wanting more coffee. I pour and ask him whether he is going to eat the slices of bread I have put out on the table for him. He doesn't react. He drinks his coffee and continues to think about something that will never completely stop worrying him. And to this sound of hot coffee being warily slurped over blue lips, I seem to have ceased to exist, or I have become an inconsequential servant, a dog they may be able to find some use for, or derive some entertainment from, should it so suit them, it certainly suits me. This was my first meeting with the Russians, and I cannot imagine how else it could have been.

4

The Russian officer's name was Oleg Illyushin and he was a colonel by rank, the commanding officer of the 759th Infantry Regiment, 163rd Division, which had advanced as far as Suomussalmi over the last week, a distance of no more than forty kilometres, a terrible week in other words, and here they were supposed to wait for reinforcements, then move west to Botnviken, cutting the country in half at its narrowest point, and breaking its back.

But I had little time to dwell on these tactics, I was put to work, the most soul-destroying slave labour I have ever been subjected to, day and night, on top of which it was also highly dangerous as the Finnish forces had in fact not left the area, but had almost surrounded the town after the Russians had occupied it, and were now ensconced in its snowbound forests around the town, shooting at everyone and everything that moved, while we were supposed to fell trees, saw and split wood, beyond the Russian lines.

To begin with, there were over forty of us, a motley workforce, engineers, lightly wounded regular soldiers and enlisted men who were too debilitated to fight, many of them not even in uniform, under the constant eye of a squat, barking quartermaster I was told the Russians called the Dog, in addition to four non-commissioned officers who treated us like prisoners, plus the interpreter, who occasionally came to ask me unanswerable questions. You could see it in all their faces, that same bottomless, senseless suffering, as their war, which had already ground to a halt after two weeks, resembled a machine that had been shot to pieces, yet running at full throttle.

I mentioned that I thought I might have seen the interpreter before, and it turned out that he had been a clerk at a sawmill in Vuokkiniemi where I had gone to cadge some offcuts a few years back. He had been studying in Leningrad at the time, and only worked at the sawmill in the summer months, a job and a place he described with great disdain, as if he were some sort of out-of-place nobleman. But he was not much of a soldier, either, not someone who followed orders, got killed, froze, starved or was brave like the others, on the contrary, he behaved as if he had some kind of right to be here, to settle an old score, maybe, a Finn and a Russian without being either. I could never work him out.

It became obvious that Illyushin, the colonel, couldn't either. At any rate there was constant friction between them, as a rule over interpretations of Finnish communications that their intelligence officers had picked up, which from time to time I was also asked to read. On these occasions they treated me like a mixture of prisoner and spy, meted out threats and punches, but friendly and ingratiating smiles, too, when I told them, for example, about the terrain around the town and the lake, the roads, the farms, distances and Finnish winters, about which they didn't have a clue. But again they argued about this, too, and had it not been for the fact that the colonel was dependent on the interpreter, he would probably have had him shot long ago, since the Russians had a habit of shooting those who were too weak to fight or work. Almost every day, there were summary court martials which previously I had only heard talk of and never believed, after all, I had known quite a few Russians in my life, good men, but now I *saw* it and had to believe it. The interpreter's name was Nikolai and he was in his late twenties, he had curly, blond hair and sallow eyes set far apart like a woodcock's, and where Colonel Illyushin had a place in his heart for the anxiety he never came to terms with, Nikolai had a tiny cavity with a void. One morning I stood watching him observe two maimed, mine-injured young boys without batting an eyelid, and I thought, that man has never had a friend, and has probably never felt the need for one.

I couldn't sleep for the first few days, and I wasn't allowed to stay in Luukas and Roosa's house. The colonel moved in, together with a number of guards and three non-commissioned officers, while the interpreter, Nikolai, and three other officers took up residence in old Babushka's newly cleaned house.

It was revolting to see because they were filthy and never did any cleaning, shat indoors, slept with their clothes on in the white beds, and in a burnt-out town there is soot, there is soot everywhere, on faces and clothes, on floors and streets and tanks and tents and cats – and it never goes away, it mixes with the powdery snow and spreads, it is swirled up in the air and melts and freezes again and eats its way into eyes and throats and noses and lungs. A burnt-out town is the filthiest of all towns in existence – it is simply that, filth.

But the house was also under a constant barrage, so after three days both the colonel and the interpreter moved out again and in to a bunker the army engineers had built between the foundations of what was left of the school, which they still hadn't covered with a roof.

I thought it a strange idea as the Finns had neither planes nor heavy artillery, and it was freezing cold in the bunker, from which red-hot stoves sent their valuable heat straight up into the air.

But the following day the Dog and his officers seemed to lose interest in us, they merely gave us stern instructions and a few guards, and then left – presumably to perform greater miracles – and they must have realised that we had nowhere to go if we were thinking of escaping. And when that same afternoon, owing to fighting to the south and east of the town, the woodcutting was brought to a complete halt and our last remaining guards disappeared, I simply left the unit and walked back to Luukas and Roosa's house and settled in, as if acting on orders.

I made a fire, heated water and washed and tidied up after the Russians until it was evening and then night, and I didn't leave again. I just went upstairs and fell into Markku's bed, Markku who was serving on the Karelian isthmus and had died on one of those very days, but I didn't know that then, I was lying in his bed, which was clean again, thinking that he was making a more courageous contribution to the Finnish war effort than I was. He died on the Taipale front, which was said to be ten times more terrible than Suomussalmi, at that point anyway, it was still only the middle of December, but now I knew the answer to a question that some seven days ago I had

had no idea it was even possible to ask – I was going to get through this. As long as it didn't become a matter of total indifference to me whether I lived or died, I couldn't distinguish one from the other, and if I had survived these first few days of all work and no sleep, I knew I would survive anything. It gave me a new sense of composure.

The next morning I turned up as usual at the Dog's parade ground, received orders and worked as before, without either the quartermaster or anyone else seeming to have missed me. When strangely enough, this day also became night, I went back to the house and continued the clean-up – there was soot everywhere. I swept and brushed and scraped and washed. I should have slept, but by now I had understood that filth and lack of sleep are two sides of the same coin, your undoing. An officer walked past, peered in and asked – as far as I could judge – what the point was, all this cleaning in the middle of a war, and he shook his head and grinned when he found out I intended to live there.

The next day the Dog reacted in the same way – if I wanted to perish, that was my business, it certainly wasn't his. And from then on I was where I was going to stay.

But work did not become any safer for that. These men weren't used to felling trees, and the patrol that was occasionally given orders to protect us wasn't exactly composed of elite soldiers: they surrounded a section of the forest, lay in the snow and waited while we moved in and blew up trees with dynamite – that was my idea – and had the horses pull them unlopped into town, it had to happen fast, and it did happen fast for as long as it lasted. A dozen huge bonfires burnt continuously around the town, the flames and white smoke merging with the grey, woollen sky. But even so the Russians didn't get their body warmth back, the cold was in their bones by now, they slept too little, washed too seldom, and food and vodka were rationed the day they arrived . . .

Then one morning a furious Nikolai informed me that 'the enemy' had managed to cut off the road which the long-awaited reinforcements were expected to use on the way to the border. A whole armoured division was stuck there now, banging their heads against a Finnish roadblock like wasps against a window, only a few kilometres outside town. We were, in other words, *totally* isolated, several thousand more men than had ever lived here before.

Illyushin continued to receive air drops of food, fuel and ammunition, but the drops often fell outside the lines, and retrieving them was extremely dangerous. We never saw anything of this 'enemy', like tiny invisible ghosts 'they' were all around us in snowdrifts day and night – and it was eerie, seeing men and horses suddenly collapse like limp rag dolls, only to hear the shots ring out long afterwards, like the muffled cries of fish from under thick ice; we lost more men each day than the Dog and his forces managed to replace. And when a large unit was pulled out to hold a critical position in Hulkonniemi, there were only seven loggers left, seven men with the task of supplying a whole town with firewood, a burnt-out, naked town beneath a lead-filled polar sky.

However, these six were good men, in their way, in their *strange* way, several of them had seen forests before and experienced freezing temperatures, if not quite thirty-five degrees below zero, and I had gradually managed to gain a kind of respect among them because I never showed any signs of fear or fatigue, with the result that on the morning we discovered we were as good as abandoned and left to our own devices, they flocked around me as though I was the last prayer of their frozen hands, a kind of hope in this war Nikolai had already started to call 'the white hell'.

With us we had a young boy of no more than seventeen from a village east of Onega who had obviously held an axe in his hands before; he was also able to control his fear and usually finished what he was given to do. I also noticed that he got enough to eat, often by stealing from the others, that he slept whenever he had the chance, and that he had a way with horses. We communicated in sign language, so well in fact that eventually he was able to translate my simple instructions. His name was Mikael; according to the interpreter he had grown up in a boys' home and had never shown any respect for either the law or the military machine that for some reason had sunk its claws into him. He was the first to call me 'the angel'. Later I was also called 'the hope', or 'the last hope', or even 'courage' and 'freedom': they were the first Russian words the war had taught me, to add to the few I had already known; there are those who believe that the Russians are scum, but that has never been my opinion, even though they are a strange lot, always have been.

Three days after we had been left on our own, confirmation came through in the morning that the officers had also begun to see me for who I was, and perhaps more especially as someone having what they themselves lacked. I hadn't had more than an hour's sleep when Nikolai personally came to wake me in Luukas and Roosa's house and told me in his shrill voice that the loggers refused to go out today, no matter what he threatened them with, I was to report to Illyushin at once.

He sat on the floor just inside the door as he said this, in order not to be shot through the frosted windowpanes, and I saw him shudder when I stood up and put on my clothes without showing the least sign of fear. In the kitchen two privates were waiting, also sitting with their backs against the wall. They wriggled their way out through the door, like worms in the grey snow. And on their way back to the bunker, they crouched and ran from the ruins of one house wall to the next, Nikolai too, while I walked in the middle of the road as though I lived there and had never done anything else, a man on his way to work at a time when God still rings his bells – not that this had anything to do with courage or reason, I can't explain it, I just knew now there was only one way to survive, my own.

I hadn't seen Illyushin for almost a week. He had red flames in what had previously been such a white face – which is usual when you constantly alternate between intense cold and great heat – he had become even thinner, seemed even more absent-minded and bewildered, and it was obvious that he was extremely reluctant to waste his time on this conversation.

He said – through Nikolai – that I was to take the loggers out with me, and *stay* out until we had enough wood for the next three days for two whole battalions, he was expecting a major offensive, and when that began, *no one*, not even we, would survive more than a few minutes beyond the lines! He finished off by saying that if I didn't arrange this, he would proceed to tear down every house in the town, and shoot the loggers, one by one.

'You like these men, don't you?'

I looked into his intense eyes as if I didn't understand what he meant and said there was no need to threaten me.

He didn't answer.

*

44

Before we went into the bunker where Mikael and his comrades were – the youngster acted as a kind of leader for them, and Nikolai knew that – the interpreter said *I* should order them out, tell them that it looked as if it would be a quiet day, that we would be accompanied by a large unit, it was absolutely imperative that we got this wood in.

I went in and repeated what he had said, as if they were my words. Nikolai pretended to be translating. It made no impression on the dejected gathering, they hardly moved. Mikael just mumbled that they would rather die in the town than out in the white hell.

Nikolai and I continued our game. I told them to stand up when I was talking to them, I explained that it was better to work than to sit here in this grave, they would be given food, and I promised to look after them with my own hands . . . and slowly but surely they stood up, Mikael first, then Suslov, a slight, nervous wreck of a man who had been a teacher in civilian life, at a primary school on Lake Ilmen, a man who, three days ago, had begun to cry and hadn't been able to stop since. I hadn't heard him utter one word in all the time we had known each other, he must have been about forty and looked more like an insect than a human being, even though, according to Nikolai, he had been a reasonably competent soldier until he broke his glasses, now he was virtually blind.

A volley of machine-gun fire tore through the tarpaulin around the watchtower and over the stockade of the fortifications, and we threw ourselves to the ground, Nikolai cursing, in both Russian and Finnish.

'How do they stay awake?' he mumbled, back on his feet and brushing the snow and splinters off his uniform.

'They sleep,' I said.

'That simple, eh?'

He looked at me with contempt.

'It is not simple. It demands iron discipline.'

I knew I had gone too far. But I also knew that we had long passed the point where he could derive any benefit from killing me. Instead we looked at each other like two fellow conspirators in a world in which neither of us belonged, and so we calmed down for a moment, then I was able to say:

'I think you should put Mikael in charge of the infantry-men you're sending out with us today. And arm him.'

'Why?'

'To keep them in order, the loggers and the soldiers.'

'I can't do that, you know that.'

'You can ask Illyushin to do it. This isn't going to be one of the quieter days.'

'He's just a kid.'

'He's more of a man than all the others here.'

The interpreter gave me a long stare, scrabbled out his tobacco pouch and lit a cigarette while the loggers stood giving each other questioning looks, waiting to see who would be the first to cave in.

'Sit down,' I said with my hands, like a priest. They glanced at the interpreter, who didn't even register what was going on, and slumped down with their heads on their knees, adopting the position they always sat in when they were neither asleep nor awake.

But Mikael stayed put, his eyes fixed on Nikolai's cigarette, the lad reminded me of a nervous marten, a mink, and had it not been for his rotund face, which seemed so out of place and bright and friendly on his slim body, he could have been a good-looking man.

'I could try,' Nikolai mumbled out of the blue, gave the cigarette to Mikael and went off.

Half an hour later he was back with the leader of the infantry unit, and he said that Mikael could not be given any kind of command, he was an unpredictable, unreliable, wild man.

'I see,' I said.

The infantryman was called Fjodor, a sergeant by rank, and couldn't have been much more than twenty. We had had him with us before, and knew that he was more concerned with protecting his own soldiers than us. He was also prone to bullying the loggers, ordering them to do things they were already busy doing – come on, come on – and exposing us to danger with his stupid ideas while he himself lay safe in the snow with his troops.

'Then you'll have to tell him,' I said, nodding towards Fjodor, 'that I think he's a coward and I don't trust him.'

Nikolai was taken aback.

'Do you mean that?'

'Yes,' I said.

'I know you *mean* it, but if I *say* that, he'll be even more difficult to deal with.'

'Do it anyway, then he'll know *you* know he's a coward, too.'

Nikolai mulled this over and remained silent.

'On your feet,' was what I thought he shouted to the loggers.

And as they got to their feet, I could hear him snarl something or other to Fjodor. The sergeant's cheeks flushed with anger, but he didn't look in my direction, so I assumed that Nikolai hadn't revealed where the displeasure originated. And as we went out to saddle up the horses, I almost thought I might have a friend in the enigmatic interpreter, or if nothing else, a signal that he wished to stay on good terms with me, which might prove useful to us both, maybe, this man was hard to fathom.

As usual, the work was like a military operation. Fjodor's soldiers split into two groups, then ran, crouched low, between tree trunks, took up positions and secured the forest so that we could move in with three men who tied dynamite to the tree trunks, while three others wound simple rubber strips around the charge so the blast would be directed into the wood and ensure the trunks were left lying with their root ends pointing towards the town.

We felled fifteen, twenty trees at a time, and waited till Fjodor gave the all-clear, which he was often cavalier about. But not today. He roared as soon as the first lot were down so that we could lead in the horses, which was the most dangerous part of the job, as we couldn't crouch and handle the huge, terrified beasts at the same time. But we could shelter behind them once we were in. So it was the horses which took the brunt of the attacks as this woodcutting procedure – as well as the field kitchens – had long been the Finns' favourite target, well, maybe even more important than the Russian positions themselves, judging by the number of salvoes. And I can't say that I would have done it any differently – take their wood and they freeze to death! Under circumstances like these, this is of course the obvious strategy any idiot would come up with. It was forty degrees below on this day, and it was to get even colder.

From the outset it had irritated me that we had to work during daylight hours, when it was dark most of the time anyway. But neither the Dog nor Illyushin sympathised with my objections, and perhaps it didn't matter, as it was even more difficult to get the loggers outside when it was dark.

All the same, I usually did what I could to delay things when we worked in daylight – came up with excuses or broke something that then had to be repaired in town, which was one of the causes for all the friction between Fjodor and me.

But this particular morning we lost two horses during the first session, Suslov broke down yet again and one of Fjodor's men was shot in the neck. The sergeant pulled back to take him to the field hospital, and immediately I made sure we had five or six unlopped trunks heaped in a hollow so that we could sit in some sort of safety and light a fire, and let the most exhausted of us sleep on a bed of spruce while Mikael and I pretended to work. We waited like this until Fjodor was back, and by then it was already afternoon and dark.

We simply disposed of the tangled heap by blowing it up, and Fjodor made no attempt to conceal his fury. But with the interpreter's threat in mind, I assume, there was no alternative but to order his men out on yet another manoeuvre.

We carried out another operation without difficulty, hearing only the odd volley in the distance, then started on yet another session, and we were well into the night before Fjodor announced that enough was enough, he was freezing to death. We did what we could not to show our relief so that it would be clear to him, and maybe to his superiors who had called off the work, this was something we did every day. It was one of the first routines we learnt, in addition to the minor acts of sabotage.

We went back to town, to the pile of tree trunks we had made that now looked like a massive, iced-up anthill. Fjodor cast his eye over it, nodded, yes, this would really have to do for this hellish day, and marched his troops back to the bunker to receive new orders, or to slink off, who knows, maybe to get some sleep while we continued to slog away, chopping up the wood, supervised now by two of the Dog's henchmen sitting by a bonfire drinking vodka, laughing and making fun of us. They were especially hard on Suslov, the half-blind teacher who nonetheless managed to stay on his feet longer than usual because he had grabbed a few hours' sleep.

5

And so the days passed. And the nights. For another four days. The loggers suffered from open frostbite wounds and severe hunger, and looked more and more like dead men, rattling husks of dried flesh staggering around, falling, weeping and fainting over stiff, frozen magpie nests of twigs, spruce branches and wood chips. At first I helped them, then I became impatient and furious with them, then I tried to erase them from my eyes and ears. But when one night we were again left to our own devices, I cocked a snook at Fjodor and the Dog and took the loggers to Luukas and Roosa's house, dressed their worst wounds and helped them into the empty beds, where they fell asleep with their clothes on before I could feed them, while Mikael and I sat on either side of the stove listening to nothing as the kitchen gradually warmed up.

'Coffee?' I asked.

He nodded, and I let him see to it, noticed his trembling face and hands, as if the water pump, the kettle, stove, wood, flames, coffee, cups . . . were a reward that was only attainable in heaven. We drank, ate, occasionally gesticulated to each other and understood what we had to say, we didn't need much language, the question that burnt like a blue flame between us, between this odd youth and myself, I couldn't answer anyway: Is this real? Somewhere, up in the polar night, we heard the drone of an aeroplane that would sound like a Russian hope, and the sound of distant shelling, which presumably meant that the Finns had deployed their artillery. But it had nothing to do with us. Here, we were sitting around a glowing stove with full stomachs and smiling at each other through the steam from two cups of coffee.

When the loggers woke, I gave them what food there was, porridge made from flour and oats, jam, pork, a little bread, and I watched them let it slither into their mouths as if they were afraid it would dissolve and slip between their ravaged fingers. No one said a word. They chewed, with slow tenacity, with their whole bodies, shot uncertain glances at one another now and then, as though they had only just become aware what company they had landed in, nodded sleepily to show they recognised each other or were sending an invisible thank-you to fate, so slowly, so slowly did they eat and nod their lice-infested heads . . . And when at last I stopped them, they looked at me like dogs and obediently returned to their beds to get more sleep, confused at not being called out to work, it was light outside the windows, wasn't it?

But I had no intention of chasing them out today.

Mikael and I went out around noon, keeping away from Illyushin's troops, but allowing ourselves to be seen by cutting wood for a field kitchen under the Dog's command. He didn't pay any attention to us, a new offensive was under way, men were running in all directions. There was chaos, clamour – and soot. We sneaked back to the house as soon as it was dark.

When we arrived, Mikael fell to his knees and thanked me, then got under Roosa's warm bedclothes and passed out again; he was on one side of the marital bed, with Suslov sleeping next to him. On seeing the teacher snoring, I remembered that Roosa had had problems with her eyes after an illness a few years ago. I started to search, in drawers and cupboards I hadn't touched before, and in the sitting room I found what I was looking for – an embroidered case and a pair of glasses with such strong lenses that just looking through them made me dizzy.

I took them in to Suslov and woke him. It took time. When eventually he saw me, I asked him to put on the glasses. He did as I said, blinked, smiled and fell asleep again, still wearing the glasses. I carefully removed them and put them next to the case on the bedside table.

There weren't many such days. Instead there was another miracle. After one offensive our camp out on the headland was evacuated and when, after a night in the open, I suggested to the Dog that the loggers could sleep in Luukas and Roosa's house, he just looked at me with that square face of his and answered as before – it was no skin off his nose if we wanted to meet our maker. From then on we arranged that, as often as the opportunity arose, we would let the weeping teacher and another wretch called Rodion sleep in the house while the rest of us worked.

Rodion was the same age as Suslov, but had worked as a mechanic in a slaughterhouse and had been far stronger before he became as weak as he was now. He had been dragged into the Red Army by Illyushin in person as the latter's division got off the train in Lietmajärvi, before the offensive began in November.

'What are you doing out of uniform, a fit man like you?' the colonel had asked when he caught sight of the civilian staring in amazement at the throngs of soldiers and vehicles streaming on to the otherwise godforsaken platform. Rodion had gone there to pick up a parcel containing a pair of shoes for his wife, unaware of the historic occasion, and now he wasn't even allowed to go home and say goodbye before having to leave, there was no uniform either, so he worked, starved and slept in the clothes he had on when he left home on 23 November, and he still carried his wife's shoes under his thin coat, day and night, as if they were the last remains of his life, wrapped in tatty pink paper covered in soot – *everything* was covered in soot, apart from these bright red shoes.

There were also two brothers in our group, a rare event in war, they were from Kiev, their names were Leo and Nadar, in their early thirties, they had another language of their own besides Russian, which they spoke to each other and none of the others understood. Leo had been a caretaker at a sewing-machine factory, and Nadar had worked on a collective farm growing cabbages, both had a game right leg, and neither was fit for active service.

In addition, we had with us a small, stocky man from Kalevala in Russian Karelia, a middle-aged, brawny Russian peasant who knew some Finnish. He had been in the Red Army reserves and had more stamina than any of them. Rodion with his shoes, Mikael the mink and this peasant, whose name was Antonov, were all used to the cold, but the brothers and the teacher were not, and even though Suslov had apparently spent a few years by Lake Ladoga in his youth, he had to be the most ill-suited man in the division, indeed in the whole war, I have never met a more peace-loving person in my life.

When the loggers had slept in the house for two nights, I managed to get their clothes off them and tried to delouse them with paraffin. I made them wash and put on clean clothes belonging to Luukas and his sons. In the course of these days they had had several meals and had caught up on their sleep, with the possible exception of Mikael, who didn't sleep any more than I did, but he didn't seem to need it, either.

But these improvements had a strange effect on the loggers, as though the food and sleep not only brought hope and strength, but also the panic that had tormented them before they gave up. And this morning they suddenly refused to go out, I had to push them, with threats and brute force, as the Dog and his corporals did. When evening came, they didn't want to sleep indoors any more either, the house was right in the line of fire, as it had been all the time. They also began – when I did finally get them inside – to fight over food, of which there was less and less every day, and Suslov didn't want to wear the glasses I had given him, they didn't fit, he said.

I told him that if he didn't put them on and wear them that evening and all the next day I would chase him back to the Dog's trench. Antonov enjoyed that, he translated it with a grin, and Suslov reluctantly put on the glasses, and wore them the next day too. And then he came to thank me, on his knees – he had got not only his eyesight back, but his strength as well. And when the brothers and Mikael got into a fight the same evening, I could see no alternative but to find Nikolai and ask him to give me a gun.

The interpreter was sitting in one of the tents drinking tea from a samovar with three other officers and jumped up as soon as he saw me, pulling me eagerly outside as if we were both privy to a secret. I could smell from his breath that he had been drinking. With a sly grin, he asked me how many men I had lost in the last twenty-four hours.

'None,' I said. 'But Fjodor has lost two.'

His smile was no more transparent.

'While we've lost over a hundred, on the road north to Juntusranta alone . . .'

There wasn't much I could say to that, and this new face of his was as inscrutable as its predecessor.

'They say you're in touch with the Finns,' he said out of the blue, taking a few uncertain steps to the side. We were standing by Babushka's house. There was a woodpile near by. I suggested sitting down. He refused.

'I'm cold,' he said, changing the subject, and shivered, distant and oblivious, but nevertheless he sank down on to the snow-covered logs and appeared to collect his thoughts before repeating his accusation.

'I don't understand what you're saying,' I answered.

'Are you in contact with the Finnish army?'

I feigned surprise.

'No.'

'So how come your men are still alive?'

'You think I've got the Finns *not* to shoot at the loggers?'

He seemed at once disappointed and furious, and now I definitely knew that he had wanted to threaten to report me, to have a hold over me, but for what purpose?

I didn't ask and, his teeth chattering, he began to talk about his life back home in Leningrad, about two sons who hadn't started school yet, about his father, who, before the revolution, had had money and a well-run spinning-mill, but who had had everything confiscated, leaving no inheritance for Nikolai and his brothers, instead the family had to live in the evil shadow of suspicion, twenty years after the revolution. It was the tale of a bitter man.

I listened and said that, as for myself, I had no family, but I had a farmstead . . .

'I have everything I need there.'

'But will you see it again?' he interrupted angrily, and stood up, swaying and trying to wag a threatening finger. '*Will you ever see it again?*'

Then he suddenly changed tack once again and broke down completely. 'I volunteered!' he sobbed. 'No one asked me, it was my own choice. I could have been lecturing in Leningrad!'

He wiped his mouth and looked at me through watery eyes as the images of these warm university rooms seemed to slip away.

'Are you never afraid?' he asked.

'No,' I said.

'That's not possible.'

He studied his hands and let them drop limply to his side. We stood motionless for a few minutes, listening to the war, the endless shelling and the invisible planes, the equally invisible enemy. I wanted to ask him about the Russian division that was supposed to be fighting its way towards the town, but managed to catch myself in time.

'The ice is thick,' he declared. 'We're making a road over the lake, going north. The trucks and tanks can take that route too.'

He paused for a moment. 'At least it's an escape route.' It just came out, a heartfelt sigh, for which he would probably have been shot if he had been in any other company than mine.

I explained that local people also often made ice roads across Lake Kiantajärvi, that Finnish soldiers knew about it and so the most stupid thing the Russians could do would be to move on to the open white expanse of ice, they would be shot to pieces, from all sides.

He looked at me wearily and nodded.

'Why am I talking to *you*? There's *something* wrong with you, isn't there.'

'Yes,' I said, hoping he wouldn't ask why I had come. Besides, the problem I had with the loggers was now fading into nothing – I had roasted some pork that evening; they had eaten with their fingers, like pigs, although I had laid out cutlery, and they wiped their hands on their new clothes, especially Rodion, with the shoes, had made a filthy mess, so I had smacked his hands against the table edge, and the others had laughed, all except Antonov, who, in his incomprehensible Finnish, had shouted that their table manners were none of my business. I had answered – calmly – that if they didn't learn to keep themselves clean they would die, of cold. But they had laughed at that, too. It was only when I forcibly shoved the cutlery into Rodion's hands and threatened to kill him that the others followed suit, first Mikael, then the teacher, and Antonov . . . the usual order, this was what Mikael's little leadership role boiled down to, being the first to understand what was worth doing, while the brothers from Kiev were the last, they never understood anything, it was a mystery to me how they had survived at all, up to now at least, but then there was a lot I didn't understand, for the moment.

But now I had the ice road to think about. Nikolai ought not to have told me about this – would he remember when he woke up and then do something to prevent me from divulging what I knew?

I looked at him and calmly told him that he could trust me, no matter what happened. I would help him back to the tent, and if he could spare a bit of food, we hadn't eaten since yesterday . . . I continued in this vein, talking and begging until we started quarrelling again, this time about food, and I didn't leave until I was certain that the ice-road was forgotten, with only *one* loaf under my arm, at the very last moment he had decided to keep the others — it serves you right, you bloody Finn, hunger has never hurt anyone.

6

The loggers were asleep when I got back. A few days earlier we had taken in a cat, it was asleep as well, in the chair where I usually sat, next to the stove. Now it woke up, sprang to the floor and waited till I had sat down before crawling back up and settling down on my lap, it was grey and had lost its tail, it seemed to have been chopped off, or blown off. I have never liked cats, but this one had got used to both us and the war, and watching it lying there curled up and licking its fur, or lapping up the drops of milk we gave it, was like revisiting a bit of the world as it used to be. The loggers were much nicer to it than they were to the horses, those great, screeching creatures that just made our miserable existence larger and more obvious than it already was, there are a lot of muscles in a horse, and a lot of blood, and it has got to come out, the whole lot, when it is blown to pieces, its strength and its blood, I love horses, I can't imagine anything more . . .

I was awoken by a loud crash, still sitting in the chair with the cat on my lap. I pushed it off, ran out and saw a large crater just a few metres away from the house, the wall had been shattered by shrapnel, but strangely enough the windows were intact. I was about to go in again when I suddenly found myself surrounded by a group of Russian soldiers. Two men grabbed hold of my arms, while the others made their way inside, screaming and shouting and dragging the loggers out of their beds and into the cold – it was an odd sight, six half-naked men with their arms above their heads, surrounded by soldiers who were lying or sitting on the ground for fear of being shot by an invisible enemy somewhere out there in the pitch darkness.

I had seen the officer in charge of the operation before, he had stayed at Babushka's house with Nikolai. He, too, was lying flat in the snow. While we had to stand and wait for twelve men to ransack the house, presumably looking for communication equipment. They didn't find anything, of course. And the officer roared an order I didn't understand. But the loggers turned and marched in a kind of goosestep towards Illyushin's command centre, hands still above their heads. I went with them.

We were met by the interpreter.

It was only hours since I had left him, a drunken wreck, now he seemed clear headed and in a good mood, almost cheerful. He began by giving the officer a dressing-down, after which the latter delivered his report, which was also received with displeasure. Nikolai bellowed a new order, and I saw the loggers react with relief – they had been given permission to go back, it was *me* all this was about.

I butted in and asked if I could say something before they left.

'What about?' Nikolai asked sourly.

I turned to Antonov and told them to tidy up when they got back, the house had to be in the same state it was before the soldiers ransacked it, or else they wouldn't see me ever again – that was a promise.

He thought it over, nodded, and left.

'What was that supposed to mean?' Nikolai asked when we were inside the tent. I didn't answer. He told me to sit down on a chair. I sat down and the officer who had fetched us bound my hands and feet. Shortly afterwards Illyushin arrived, threw a brief glance in my direction, said a few words in Russian and was gone. The officer began to hit me in the face, first with his fists and then with a rifle butt. Nikolai lit a cigarette and waited until the man had been at it for a while.

'Does it hurt?' he asked.

'Yes,' I said. 'But I am strong.'

He gave a scornful laugh.

'I can have him continue.'

'What for?'

'To make you talk.'

'You only have to ask. I'll talk.'

'Then explain to me how that damned house of yours is still standing,' he yelled, as hysterical as the time when we were sitting on the woodpile and the saliva was drooling from his mouth.

'I can't,' I said. 'But there are other houses in the town in the same state as when you arrived.'

'They burnt down the whole town!' he screamed. 'And are you trying to tell me that they let just a few houses stand, let them stand when they could have blown the whole lot to smithereens, is *that* what you want me to believe?'

'Perhaps they knew there was no one in them,' I said, thinking about the Finnish soldier who couldn't bring himself to set fire to Babushka's house.

'How could they know no one was living in them,' came the triumphant rejoinder, 'if no one had told them?'

I tried to smile, but my mouth was full of blood, the left side of my face as numb as ice.

'They're too exposed for that,' I said. 'No one would dream of living in them, not even . . .'

'So we can just move back in, can we,' came the retort, still triumphant. But now I was beginning to have difficulty speaking.

'Smoke from the chimneys,' I managed to mumble.

'Does it hurt?' he asked.

'No.'

The blood bubbled in my mouth. He motioned to the officer, who laid into me again. I blacked out for a moment and saw two new officers when I came to again. I straightened up. Nikolai was standing with his back to me, laughing at something or other. One of the newcomers pointed out that I was conscious; he turned and said something in Russian.

'I told them you don't think it hurts,' he said. 'They think that's interesting.'

I heard subdued laughter.

'Smoke from the chimneys,' I mumbled again, hardly able to make him out through the red mist. But his voice was clear.

'So they know no one is living in the houses because there is no smoke coming from the chimneys?'

I nodded.

'But there is smoke coming from *one* chimney,' he roared. 'From *yours*. And they know there's a Finn living in the town, an idiot. They put two and two together and work out that it must be the idiot who lives in the only house with a fire going, because he is the only one stupid enough to do that.'

I tried to smile. I couldn't. But he noticed the attempt.

'Do they know you're here at all?!' he yelled, banging his hands down on the arms of the chair.

'Yes,' I said. 'They let me stay.'

'Why?'

'I refused to leave.'

He moved away and swore, obviously dissatisfied at having heard an explanation that was plausible, even to him.

The next time I came to, only the officer who had beaten me was present; he was sitting on a chair next to me, smoking. When he realised I was conscious, he got up and went to fetch Nikolai, who came in and glanced disdainfully at me. He said something to the officer, who untied the knots around my wrists and ankles. I sank to the floor, but struggled to my knees.

'Do you know why you're no danger to us?' Nikolai said, his face again twisted in triumph. 'Which makes it possible for me to let you go?'

'No.'

'*I'm* the only person you can talk to!'

I nodded to show that I understood, even though at first I didn't, but it must have had something to do with his confidences, about the blockade to the east of the town and the ice road he had described as an escape route, all those things that I wouldn't be able to betray. But why didn't he just get rid of me, make sure I couldn't say anything in Finnish either? Was it because he had a private plan, held in reserve, separate from the military madness he was part of, and I might be of some use?

'So the Finnish idiot can go back and stoke the fire to his heart's content, and we'll see who . . .'

He didn't finish the sentence.

I staggered out and rubbed snow on my face. But I couldn't walk, and the house was so far away that my hands and knees were also in a state by the time I arrived. The loggers were sitting there, waiting. Mikael and Suslov fell to their knees beside me and wept when I fell across the doorstep. Antonov helped me up into the chair by the stove. The brothers set to work, tending to my wounds, their hands thorough and gentle. Rodion, with the shoes, said something that Antonov brushed aside and refused to translate, presumably because it was sentimental.

'We didn't think you would be coming back,' the stocky peasant said when the brothers were finished. 'But now you're back after all, and we have tidied up.'

He motioned towards the newly cleaned kitchen. I nodded to signify that I had registered the fact, and was pleased with them.

'What did you tell them?' he asked.

'The truth,' I said in Russian.

He thought about that and smiled.

I saw by the clock hanging between the family photographs that daylight was still a few hours away. I ordered Antonov to wake me before daybreak and said we would have to work hard in the time ahead, it was our only chance. It was evident that he wanted to ask why, but I stopped him by pretending I had a secret he would not benefit from knowing.

He translated for the others and stood looking at me, pondering yet another question.

'Why didn't they kill you?' he asked.

'I don't know,' I said.

Shortly afterwards I fell asleep.

7

I managed to keep going for most of the day, despite dizziness, aching gums and the fact that my face was so swollen I could hardly see.

But the loggers worked as never before. Suslov wore his glasses and had stopped fumbling and falling, Antonov and Mikael worked together like father and son, Rodion had left the red shoes in the house and swung the axe like a young man, while the brothers spoke Russian, and only that – they were finally a team, now I was the only one who was no use.

We had been assigned a new unit to protect us, with a leader who turned a blind eye when I stretched out next to a bonfire for a few hours. He even offered me a cigarette, which I accepted and gave to Mikael as soon as his back was turned.

When darkness fell, the unit left us without any explanation, and Mikael slunk off to steal some food. As usual, luck was on his side and he came back with two whole loaves, it was no more than a day's rations for four men, but we still had some pork fat we could melt in a pan, cool in the snow and use as a spread. Strangely enough, the soldiers who ransacked the house hadn't found the remaining jam and coffee, and I think we were the only section in Suomussalmi on this evening so close to Christmas 1939, sitting and drinking hot coffee in a warm house — as usual, the loggers were grateful to have survived yet another day, and as usual they thanked me, the only person not to be of any use. Rodion even thought it had to be the first day since he had left Ledmozero that he hadn't felt the cold.

'You're learning,' I said.

Antonov grinned and said that he had already told him that.

'Let's hope he doesn't go and forget it all.'

But I had noticed something as we were walking back from the forest: smoke rising from the chimneys of several of the houses left standing, Babushka's and the three houses closest to ours. I didn't say anything to the elated loggers. Our officer had mentioned that we would have to reckon on being picked up some time that evening because another offensive was imminent. But the hours passed as we sat and rested and slept like corpses without anything happening. Around midnight Antonov woke me up and asked in a whisper what we should do – in all this stillness, if no one came to collect us.

I had my eyesight back, and some of the swelling in my face had gone down, only my nose was still sore, but I was just as dizzy.

I got up and went out into the starry night and saw that smoke was still coming out of the four chimneys, not distinct, slender columns like the smoke from our chimney – we used dry spruce – but heavy, yellow smoke from green wood. I went back in and woke Mikael, asked Antonov to order him to check the houses with the smoking chimneys, to find out whether anyone was living there. The young lad couldn't see what good it would do, but he went anyway, came back an hour later – with another loaf – and said no one was living in the houses, but he had seen two soldiers enter one of them and leave immediately afterwards, and straight away thick smoke could be seen rising from the chimney; he said in passing that the town was strangely quiet, you would almost think it had been evacuated.

Antonov frowned and looked at me, asked whether we should wake the others and get ready, but I decided that as long as no one came for us, we should stay put, I needed another night, at least, for my hands and my eyes. They didn't say so, but I could see they were both relieved, even though the silence grew and grew as the hours passed – we had been having storms for more than two weeks; now we could suddenly hear the frost in the forest and the stars in the sky.

But the grey dawn broke and neither Fjodor nor the Dog nor the new officer appeared. However, the war had burst into life again. It had also moved closer. I decided that we should still stay indoors, and the loggers went back to sleep, again without a word of protest, while I made myself comfortable in the chair by the stove, and sat there all day listening to something coming closer and closer, with a mutilated cat on my lap. It also slept. I decided to call it Mikke.

Then it grew dark and still no one came.

I made coffee and went to rouse the others. Mikael looked at me as if he were waking to a summer's day in his home village by Lake Onega, the brothers emerged from sweet dreams about Kiev, Antonov blinked his eyes cheerfully and folded his hands across his chest, even the teacher seemed at peace. For the first time more than monosyllabic words issued from his mouth. I patted him on the shoulder and handed him a cup of coffee, he sat up, slurped a few mouthfuls and continued to talk, the way a teacher should, I suppose, an even stream of words ending in a question mark, I could hear that from the intonation, and his eyes, which looked at me as though I had become his closest confidant, a man to beg for patience and mercy.

I told him to get up and fetch the others. We gathered in the kitchen for a kind of military officers' meeting. There was no longer any doubt as to who the leader was; rebellions, fights, disagreements – those were things of the past. I took the decision there and then that we should continue to stay in the house, keep the fire going and rest, eat what food we had left, and if need be send Mikael out for more. Sooner or later something was going to happen, and then I would know what we should do, for the time being it would have to be my secret – at least that was one way of maintaining calm, both in them and myself.

I watched them closely as Antonov translated, and I saw them each nod in turn, composed and resolute, as if we had been planning a conquest – all we needed was some time to prepare. Mikael was the only one to say something.

'Have they forgotten us? The Dog and the interpreter . . . ?'

'They've just got other things to do. But it doesn't matter, we can rest.'

Then I urged them to stay calm, I had to go out, but I would be back.

They nodded, and even looked shamefaced.

I looked at the cat lying on the chair.

'I came back last time,' I said. 'I'll be back this time, too.'

The same nodding. Before I left I whispered to Antonov that he should keep an eye on the teacher.

*

A barrage of flares illuminated the night sky, black figures slithered nervously among the ruins, the armoured positions behind the stumps of walls around the centre of the town were lit up, the huge, black grubs stood facing the northern and eastern perimeters of the town, firing off occasional volleys into the forest. As before, on the shore close to Hulkonniemi total war was taking place, with the same unclear picture of Russian MG posts and artillery blasting salvo after salvo into the forests and across the ice. 'Enemy' shellfire was coming closer like the stitches of a gigantic sewing machine, screams of pain, shouted commands and whistling medics – the machine was running amok, and a billowing carpet of brown smoke settled across the town, so dense and boundless that it enveloped the sky as well, and there we sat, in the middle of all this, like maggots in the core of a rotten apple.

The tent where Nikolai had interrogated me was burnt to the ground. I heard voices from the bunker in the old school and noticed that the store of wood by Babushka's house was almost gone. The command centre's field kitchen stood cold and abandoned while the woodpile by Antti's shop was as good as untouched. But I had no idea how to interpret these changes, which actually didn't change anything at all, so when I went back I told the loggers we should eat at our leisure and get a bit more sleep.

Once more they eyed me with doubt. Once more their protests remained unspoken. And after a wordless meal they each went to their beds, and slept, while I made do with the chair in the kitchen and the cat.

In the middle of the night, Antonov woke me up, he said he couldn't sleep any longer and waved his hands about to signify either illness or confusion.

'What's happening out there?'

'I don't know.'

But I added that we shouldn't worry, all that mattered was that we would be strong and rested when something did happen, whatever it might be, evacuation, rout, bombardment . . . we would be ready and strong, that was all. And, to distract him, I asked how the teacher was doing since he had been raving in his sleep.

'He's doing fine,' the peasant mumbled, but with an expression that said as fine as a miserable creature like him could do.

I said that Suslov was strong and he would surprise us. Sceptical, Antonov shrugged his shoulders.

'Just wait,' I continued, as though we had bet money on how Suslov would act. The peasant just shrugged again, gave me a resigned look and went back to bed.

The next morning the same thing happened – no Fjodor and no Dog, either. But during the course of the morning the war intensified. We had to yell at each other to be heard. I made coffee for the loggers and said we wouldn't be doing anything today apart from sleeping and waiting, or if need be sending Mikael out for food.

But now the young lad had had enough; he liked going out, but first he wanted to know if the house had a cellar.

I nodded and listened to the heated discussion that broke out among them. When they had calmed down, Antonov asked if I would give them permission to carry the mattresses down to the cellar.

'Yes,' I said, 'but it's cold. And it's no safer than up here.'

Antonov translated and a new debate ensued – the brothers were the ones who were most in favour of going to the cellar. I told Antonov to say there was no point taking precautions that had no point. He grimaced and said he didn't understand what I meant and therefore refused to translate.

I said it was just as dangerous in the cellar as in the house, but it was easier to escape from the house.

He shrugged and nodded towards the brothers, as if to say it was impossible to stop their fussing. But by now the others had finally managed to calm themselves down, even Suslov seemed resigned to yet another night – *upstairs*.

In the end they went back to their beds while the brothers carried their mattresses down to the cellar. But, in the middle of the night, they came back up again and slept on the kitchen floor, like dogs at their master's feet. I pretended I was asleep and could hear Leo crying and Nadar telling him off. Then it was quiet, in the house and outside, a silence that lasted for so long that once more I thought I had gone deaf. Mikael and Antonov came down as night was turning to day and said that now they *had* to know what was going on.

'They've evacuated the town!'

'No, the Finns are probably regrouping. We won't find out if this is to our advantage until they start shooting again.'

They exchanged bewildered glances.

'Are they preparing for a final onslaught?'

I repeated that I didn't know and added that there was no point thinking about it. Again Antonov seemed not to understand.

Then, with a little smile, I asked if he *hoped* the Finns would take the town *before* we got out? And he looked even more bewildered. I laughed again and asked whether he had considered at all what might happen to us, what options we had, what a tight spot we were in and what pinpoint timing we would need, whatever we did. I mentioned something about the eye of a needle, and Mikael laughed, although he didn't understand what I was saying.

They went to wake the others and held council, in excited whispers, afraid I would hear. In the end they carried their mattresses and bedclothes down to the cellar, without so much as a glance in my direction.

Meanwhile, I stayed in the chair in the kitchen.

Only when daylight seeped in through the icy windows did the fighting flare up again. And the sounds had certainly changed, but it was still impossible to understand what that might mean, for us. Shortly afterwards, the loggers came back up, shivering and ashamed, gathered around the stove and said they hadn't had a wink of sleep, it was worse than working in the forest, it was worse than being shot at. Antonov pointed to his head to demonstrate that the brain alone was capable of destroying what even a war could not.

'Go back to your beds,' I said.

They stared at me in disbelief.

'Shouldn't we go out *now?*'

Despair shone from their faces.

'No,' I said coldly. 'If the house is still standing by the time it gets dark, I'll go and find out what's happening. If it *isn't* standing, there's nothing more to think about.'

It was now close on three days and nights since they had left the house. But I had needed this time, every hour of it, my hands had healed, I could see through both eyes, although the left one, I could feel, was watering a little. And once more the loggers did as I told them.

8

Before the previous lull the shells had been landing in the street in front of the house and in the burnt-out ruins to the west of us. Now they were falling in the forest to our rear, across the fields and in a semicircle radiating out from the church ruins where Illyushin had positioned his heaviest artillery. If we had been in a blind spot before, we were certainly in another one now.

Without a word to the loggers, I left the house and made it safely to the command post, where a soldier sprang up and pointed his rifle at me. I raised my hands in the air and calmly stared at him until he recognised me. He waved the barrel about and tried to chase me into the bunker. But the next moment something exploded only a few metres behind us, and he ran out again. I squeezed down on to a wooden bench and sat for almost half an hour before Nikolai came out with a wounded officer.

I stood up and was subservient.

'I have come for new orders,' I said.

'Orders?' said the interpreter absent-mindedly, as if he didn't recognise me, and then carried on talking to the wounded officer, who straight afterwards limped down to his post.

'We haven't done a stroke of work for several days,' I said. 'So I was thinking . . .'

He tried to stop me, but there was no holding me back. 'We haven't seen Fjodor for several days either, nor the quartermaster, nor the section that was with us.'

He stood thinking for a while. Yet another shell struck the ground outside, snow and splinters of wood rained down on us, he didn't notice. Nikolai had been clean, well groomed and impeccably shaved for the first few days, a credit to both himself and the corps, now he wasn't a credit to anyone.

'Fjodor has deserted,' he said, and slumped down on the bench, muttering that the sergeant had simply disappeared, together with the whole of his wretched unit, no doubt hoping they would be able to find their way back across the border. 'The idiots!' he concluded, hardly able to light his cigarette.

'Perhaps they'll surrender to the Finns?' I suggested.

He didn't seem to hear.

'If the Forty-fourth don't manage to break through soon, we're as good as . . .' He held the smoke in his lungs. '. . . wiped out,' he finished, looking into my eyes, seemingly without a thought of the beating he had inflicted on me. 'But that's not why you came, to ask for orders, is it?'

'Yes, it is,' I said, but I also wanted to hear what was going on in the houses where he had started to fire up the stoves, whether anyone lived there, or whether he just wanted to force the Finns into blowing them to bits, not to mention finding out whether they were habitable – those were the two explanations I could think of, and it all looked like one big muddle, just like the war we were embroiled in, but I couldn't say that, I realised, as there was something else I wanted to find out, something I brought up when he wouldn't say anything about the houses.

'I've been thinking about what you told me about the ice road,' I said. 'You mustn't use it.'

His mouth fell open.

'What are we supposed to do, then!' he shouted, jumping to his feet. 'Stay here all winter? Have you the slightest idea how many men we lost last night alone?!'

Without warning, he pressed me up against the parapet and snarled that if I so much as mentioned that cursed ice road again, or anything else for that matter, he would have me shot so full of holes that not even God would recognise me.

I could tell by his grip that he wasn't particularly strong, which I had already suspected, but I let him carry on until he was finished, it took time.

'You haven't even painted your tanks white,' I said, pursuing the same line, and he flared up again.

'You want to send us straight into a trap with this stupid advice of yours! That's what! You want us to stay here! Or you want us on the ice. It all comes to the same thing!'

Finally he seemed to hear what he was saying, it was similar to what I had said about the houses, everything and everyone was stuck here. But then he pursed his lips and suddenly seemed clear headed, he sat down, slapped his knees and ordered me to sit on the bench beside him.

'You *can't* help us,' he declared, blowing smoke through his teeth.

'No,' I said.

'That would be treachery,' he continued. 'And you are no traitor.' He chuckled. 'You're a funny one, but you're no traitor, you're a logger!'

That was the first time I had heard his real laugh.

'Yes,' I said.

He grew serious again.

'But just let's suppose I pass on this advice of yours, what do you think my superior officers will say?'

I shrugged, and for a moment he seemed to notice my mutilated face.

'As a matter of fact, that doesn't matter,' he said, changing his tune and leaning against the shattered parapet.

In the course of the few weeks we had known each other I had never seen him more apathetic, weary, demoralised, filthy and lacking in anything remotely resembling courage – he looked like the loggers before they returned from the dead.

'I know what you're after,' he went on. 'But we haven't given up. *I* haven't given up!'

'I know that,' I said. 'But whatever happens, we'll have to go out tomorrow, there's hardly any firewood left in town.'

'Well, *go* out, then! Do what you like!'

That was only half of the answer I was after.

'Will we get any protection?'

He gave a bitter laugh.

'You can see for yourself what things are like here.'

'Are you expecting another offensive – tonight, tomorrow?'

'What sort of question is that? There are offensives here all the time, we're right in the middle of one now.' He drew breath. 'Yes,' he conceded, 'we're expecting a new offensive.'

'Then I'll wait another night,' I said, and got up.

'Do that,' he mumbled, stubbing out his cigarette.

'But I think that will be it after that,' I said, to emphasise that I might be talking about something other than cutting wood, and I stood bent over him as I said it, and could have killed him with a single blow of my fist.

'I see,' was all he said as, wearily, he looked away.

'What day is it today?' I asked.

'The twenty-fourth . . . no, the twenty-eighth . . .'

I imagined he might be the most difficult to deal with if I decided to take him along with me, not just because now he was more drained than the loggers, but also because he had responsibility, was an officer – he may have had the fear of a slave, but he didn't have the freedom of a slave, as the loggers did, and yet: why did I need him? Because *he* needed *me*? It struck me that this was a question I hadn't asked myself before, I was groping in the dark, just like him, we were sitting here rambling on, both of us hoping the other would understand and not understand, while the nightmare was ripping my forests to shreds. We were an impossible pairing – he was a man whose mind I would never be able to see into, we were exactly the same.

'Now I've told you,' I said. 'Now you know.'

'I don't,' he said.

'I must have food,' I said.

'You can have vodka,' he said, getting up with a groan. He went out and returned with a canteen and three loaves, and threw in a grimace of pure contempt for good measure, self-contempt.

The loggers were up and in the kitchen – fighting. Rodion and the brothers from Kiev were fighting while the others sat around laughing and cheering. I managed to separate them, but had to be rough with Nadar. I didn't want to do this, he squealed like a sick animal and played hurt, like a child. Then I saw he was clasping something to his chest, a shoe. Rodion threw himself at him again and snatched it off him, kicked him in the face and ran into the sitting room.

'I only wanted to *hold* it,' Nadar whimpered as the others roared with laughter.

At first Antonov wouldn't say a word about what had happened. I went out and fetched an axe, found Rodion lying in a chair and sobbing, dragged him back into the kitchen, asked who wanted to die first, screamed that it would be Antonov if he didn't translate, at *once*!

They stared at me, aghast.

'We're going out,' I said.

Antonov stammered a translation. 'But first we have to collect all the clothes in the house we can find and spread them out on the floor,' I continued. 'Then *I* will decide who is going to wear what, and everything else we have to do, too.'

They dutifully started searching. And when I had shared out the clothes, I asked Antonov to translate for the others that Mikael and I were going to look for skis – there might well be a few pairs left in the town. They nodded without making a comment. Nadar had resumed the same sly grin that often suffused his blank face when he spoke the secret language with his brother. I held the axe in front of his eyes and waited until he had sat down and begged for mercy. Then I told Antonov to look after them and the teacher to check what food we had left and then pack it in two rucksacks.

We searched for several hours, and found only two pairs of skis, one of which had belonged to a child, and none of our boots fitted the bindings. We also came across a little sled. Mikael managed to find two more loaves, and in the ruins of a house the Russians had abandoned we found ten or so helmets, five packets of army biscuits and an enormous roll of bandages. We left the helmets and packed everything else into the sled.

On the way back we walked straight into a summary court martial. Four soldiers with bared heads – presumably deserters – were lined up along a ditch not far from the field hospital. At a signal from an officer I recognised from Illyushin's bunker, a machine gun mowed them down, and they fell into the ditch without uttering a sound. Mikael started to tremble. When we arrived back at the house I asked him to wait outside, went in to fetch Antonov and ordered him to tell the young lad not to breathe a word of what we had seen to the others.

'What has he seen?' the peasant asked, staring hard at me, and again I thought that this wasn't going to work without language, or weapons, which meant Nikolai. But Mikael nodded obediently and looked at me with that wise-predator look of his, so I postponed the impossible decision once more and went inside to see to the skis, and try to work out how I should go about keeping them housebound for another twenty-four hours, perhaps even longer, the time it would take for the eye of the needle to open.

9

I gave the loggers a variety of jobs – keeping the fire going, repairing tools, washing and cleaning, I told them we had to leave the house in the same tidy condition we had found it. Then I acted as if I was interested in getting to know as much as possible about them, it was important to find out what they could and couldn't do, I said, Antonov interpreting this to the best of his ability.

But I noticed that there were certain things he wasn't translating. And now the teacher had started to speak again, calmly and convincingly, from his shattered lectern.

'What's he saying?' I asked as he went on endlessly. But Antonov was quick to say: 'Nothing.' And it was my impression that this reluctance wasn't due to translation problems, but to the teacher.

'Right,' I said. 'Translate.'

The peasant rolled his eyes.

'He's talking about a student of his who stole a horse . . .'

'Yes?'

Undeterred, Suslov kept talking, an enigmatic smile on his face, rattled off a long sentence and waited for Antonov, who took three times as long to translate it. Then the teacher continued while the others listened; when he said something funny, they suppressed their laughter until Antonov had translated it so that we could all laugh together; when he said something profound, they nodded reverently at every Finnish word spoken – a boy, one of Suslov's students, had once stolen a horse and ridden it to the next town to sell it. But he was found out and arrested. However, during the questioning he told them he hadn't stolen the horse to get money for his family, the foreman at the factory where his father worked had forced him, and he stuck to this explanation, no matter how many times he was beaten.

The foreman was called in and he denied the accusation. But people thought it unlikely that a boy of twelve could persist with a lie for so long, so they trusted him. An investigation was carried out, and they found that the foreman had been pocketing company money, cooking the books, and had also had an annexe built on to the already very attractive house where he lived. Accordingly, he was arrested and sentenced, not just for fraud but also for horse theft, which he had not actually committed. And the boy was not only acquitted, he also received a reward.

Suslov paused, with a contented look on his face.

'What's the point?' asked Nadar when the story showed no signs of progressing. The teacher smiled and told him to guess, as if he were addressing a slow student. That irritated Nadar. Suslov, however, knew he was on safe ground.

'You're stupid and ignorant,' he said, wagging an out-stretched finger. 'Of course, it's much more difficult for a child to lie than it is for an adult.'

'But he did?'

'Yes, he behaved as immorally as an adult.'

The teacher crossed his arms, and there was a brief silence.

'But some good came of it in the end, didn't it?' Leo said, coming to his brother's rescue. 'The rogue was caught, wasn't he.'

'Yes, but that doesn't make it just,' Suslov said, by now obviously irritated. 'No one should . . .'

'What *is* justice?' Mikael shouted. 'That was just in my eyes.'

'You say that because you don't know any better. In a civilised country, you see, the boy would have received his punishment as well. And the foreman would have been caught much earlier.'

The loggers eyed each other and a heated exchange followed, which Antonov made no attempt to translate. I ordered him to tell them that *I* would decide what was just and what was not.

'But he's a Jew,' Antonov protested in Finnish, pointing with contempt at Suslov, who clearly understood what had been said and unleashed a long, passionate tirade. The others began to laugh, Antonov, too. 'Now he says he's a gypsy,' he whinnied.

Evidently Suslov understood that, too, and he protested with renewed fury. When he had finished, Antonov explained that the teacher had only said he was a gypsy as an example.

'An example of what?'

'He didn't say. He wanted to demonstrate something.'

Suslov screamed.

'Now he says we're more stupid than even Russians are. He's angry.'

'I can see that. Is he really a Jew?'

'No, no, no!' bellowed the teacher.

'Do you understand Finnish?' I asked. 'Ask him if he knows any Finnish.'

Antonov asked the question, and Suslov collapsed on a chair with his hands in front of his face. The others started to talk among themselves; I thought I heard something about cigarettes and vodka. But then the teacher jumped to his feet again.

'Just two months later the boy stole another horse!' Antonov translated with enthusiasm. The loggers clapped their hands and everyone laughed in unison.

'Did he want to sell that one too?'

The teacher gave Mikael a desperate look.

'That's neither here nor there. He'd been ruined, *that's* what the story teaches us, he'd been corrupted.'

The others waited patiently for Antonov to finish translating, then they sat still, I suppose, expecting me to say something. I didn't. Then the youngest brother repeated what everyone else had on their mind.

'Did he try to sell this horse, too?'

'Yes,' the teacher said in a flat voice, and made a show of closing his mouth.

'He doesn't want to go on,' Antonov said.

Annoyed, the loggers protested and begged. Nadar stood up and threatened to kick him. The teacher jumped up again, and now even I understood.

'I'm saying nothing! You idiots!'

'He's calling us idiots! You, too!' Antonov screamed, pointing at me.

'Me?'

The peasant nodded.

'Yes, he said *the Finn, too*.'

94

Then Mikael said something under his breath which obviously embarrassed the teacher.

'Mikael didn't say anything,' Antonov hastened to say, folding his arms in front of his chest.

'Yes, he did,' I said. 'And you're going to translate!'

'I refuse.'

I walked over to the wood basket, picked up the axe, put it down on the table and said that Antonov had one minute to translate what Mikael had said.

'I'll start counting now. . .'

Anxious, the peasant glanced at the boy, then looked down.

'He threatened to kill him if he didn't continue the story,' he said dispassionately, and lowered his eyes, as though agreeing that they should put the teacher under real pressure. I noticed the others staring at us.

'We must help each other,' I said.

Antonov looked up, a question in his eyes.

'Shall I translate that?'

'Yes.'

'But we want to hear the story!'

'I didn't realise your Finnish was so good,' I said, and again he looked at me, puzzled, then he inclined his head in a proud gesture of acknowledgement.

'I know a lot. But now we want to hear the rest of the story. That's only right!'

I agreed. At the same time I feared that conceding could weaken my authority, and the teacher was obviously eager to know what we were talking about. I pushed the axe across the table, grabbed his hands and placed them on the shaft.

'Tell him to defend himself!'

Once more Antonov sent me a questioning look, but he did as I said, and Suslov let go of the axe as if it were burning hot.

'He says he's got nothing to defend,' the peasant laughed.

'Then he'd better tell the story.'

Antonov braced himself and yelled into the face of the teacher, who keeled over backwards. The others roared with laughter.

I helped Suslov back on the chair and gesticulated that he didn't have a choice. But when he did finally begin to speak, his voice was mechanical, passionless, like a reading in an empty church. The loggers were angry.

'He's sabotaging the story,' Antonov said, and wound himself up to yell again. Mikael beat him to it, probably repeating the threat to kill the teacher. Suslov, in desperation, waved his arms about and babbled on.

'Now he says when the boy received a reward instead of a punishment that was the end of the story, that's all we can learn from it. What do *you* think?'

'Why did he tell us that the boy stole another horse, then?'

Antonov repeated the question. Suslov answered like a condemned man.

'He says we forced him into it.'

'So it's not true?'

'Yes, it is true, but it only proves that the boy really had been corrupted, that is what he thinks, and now he wants to be left in peace, but I think he's hiding something.'

The first time I saw Antonov I thought there was something wrong with him, the way there is something frightening about an animal which, from birth, behaves differently from all the others, after all, you don't expect a dog to sing or a blackbird to bleat, and ever since we had met, Antonov had looked as if he were working at home in his fields, with a pitchfork and a hoe on a beautiful, peaceful summer's day, and that was impossible – we had become unrecognisable even to ourselves over these weeks, all of us, and now, for the life of him, he couldn't let go of this story.

'I think he's disgusting,' he persisted, nodding towards the teacher. 'And I'm sure he's a Jew. *Both* a Jew and a gypsy. I've heard it's possible.'

I repeated that he spoke excellent Finnish, even though there were mistakes in every single sentence.

'It's tiring,' he said in a conciliatory tone, and flexed his arms to suggest hard graft. The teacher used the opportunity to lie down on the bench next to the water buckets. At that moment the ground beneath us trembled, cups and glasses fell out of the cupboards, and both the windows facing the street were blown in.

I made sure no one was hurt, ran out and saw that the nearest house had taken a direct hit, one of those Nikolai had lit a fire in – the roof and one wall were ablaze, and shadowy figures with rifles accompanied by a medic with a rolled-up stretcher were running through the ruins. Seconds later, Illyushin's artillery retaliated while the tanks positioned around the church ruins began to scatter and grind their way north.

I ran up the hill towards Babushka's house and saw that it was still standing, dark and abandoned. But a dozen or so soldiers streamed out of nearby houses and disappeared into the nearest trenches. Five or six men were trying to put out a fire in a field kitchen, privates and officers were running back and forth, you couldn't hear yourself think, and for the very first time I saw flashes of light from the forest on the other side of the lake, Finnish gunfire, they were right down by the ferry landing.

I made my way back to the loggers, who were still lying on the kitchen floor, panic stricken, picking splinters of glass and wood from their hair and clothes, all except Mikael, who was busy nailing planks across the blown-in windows while repeating the same sentence over and over again, like a maniac.

'He keeps saying he isn't dead,' Antonov said. 'What shall we do?'

'I don't know.'

We sat listening in silence to the war until we thought the sounds had returned to what they once were.

'I think it's Christmas,' Antonov said out loud.

'Yes,' I said. 'That was yesterday . . .'

He thought about it.

'Finnish Christmas?'

I nodded.

'Are we going to survive?' he asked.

'Yes,' I said.

He thought about that, too.

'But you don't *know*, do you,' he said, squeezing out a smile.

I tried to smile back.

'They're evacuating the town,' I said. 'They're done for.'

Antonov shouted a few sentences in Russian; the others stared at us anxiously.

'What about us?'

'I don't know.'

'What will the Finns do to us?'

'I don't know that, either.'

Rodion was squat, thick-set, even in such an emaciated condition, a physically strong mechanic with a strange head and sitting with a pair of ladies' shoes clasped to his chest.

'We're not wearing uniforms,' he mumbled. 'Perhaps they'll think we're prisoners, or deserters. You can explain that to them, can't you?'

'If the Russians let us stay,' I said, 'I don't know what the Finns will think of us. And nor do we know what the town will be like when they recapture it, if there's anything left of anything . . .'

I began to tell them about my farmstead twenty kilo-metres north of the town, on the eastern shore of Lake Kiantajärvi, in Lonkkaniemi, told them that if we worked together, we might be able to get there, lie low until it was over, there was enough food and firewood . . . I kept talking while my brain tried to repress the question of how I would get these bags of bones across more than twenty kilometres of snow, metres deep, at forty degrees below, without being seen by Russians or Finns, who were close to both sides of the lake. Leo began to speak.

'He says we should take the sheets and make our-selves ghost costumes,' Antonov smiled. 'Then they won't see us.'

'I thought the same,' I lied, annoyed that it wasn't my idea; the house was full of bedlinen, white as snow, there was a sewing machine here, too. The brothers both spoke at once, trying to persuade the others.

'They say we should risk it,' Antonov said. 'And I agree. Perhaps we could take some of the horses with us?'

I thought about the idea, busily trying to find a way to win time.

'What does the teacher think?'

Antonov exchanged a few words with Suslov. The teacher nodded, and Antonov said he agreed. I looked at Mikael. Antonov said he, too, agreed, although the boy didn't look as if he knew what to think. We looked at Rodion, who was lying on a rag rug with his hands folded over his face, his skull gleaming red in the glow from the door of the wood burner and his thumbs drumming against his eyelids.

'*Da*,' he said without looking at us. '*Da!*'

They were like a gang of children who had just got their own way, and taking no notice of a deafening crash that blew out the window on the east wall, we started to trawl the house for bedlinen, carried Roosa's sewing machine into the kitchen. The brothers cut the cloth and Rodion and the teacher sewed — they were all talking at the same time, bickering, joking, laughing, and were not in the slightest bit interested in the pandemonium outside. But at least now we would be busy for most of the night, we hoped. We only had this one eye of the needle — how long was it since Suomussalmi had been set ablaze? Three weeks, four, a whole lifetime. But then there were further problems with the brothers, who wanted to set off as soon as the costumes were finished, and Suslov, who for some reason had become the group's boldest champion of this reckless plan. It was only thanks to a desperate scream that I was able once again to force Antonov to restrain them.

It was light for only a few hours, it was just as cold, shells exploding, screams, tank tracks biting into the crust of the frozen ground, vehicles bursting into flames, ablaze and lifeless, trees reduced to splinters and toppling over streets and troop positions, and men running everywhere. The town held — and the only thing we could do was what we were doing, nothing.

I had packed the windows with pillows and bedding, kept the fire ablaze in the kitchen, where I stayed with the cat and Mikael and Antonov, who took it in turns to sleep, probably to keep an eye on me. Antonov had pulled out a knife and sat next to the stove carving a piece of wood, sporadically mumbling a few words to himself, his enormous shoulders quivering when something or other fell close by. The loggers had sewn pointed hoods on the costumes, we looked like white monks.

'It's unbelievable,' he said.

'What is?'

'That they haven't hit the house.'

I nodded. He stopped carving and looked at me.

'What do you think about in good times?' he asked.

I didn't understand what he meant, there were four mistakes in the sentence, but he repeated the question, and I could see that we had to talk.

'The forest,' I said, just to say something. And he chuckled, as if he had never heard anything so stupid. 'The forest has wonderful sounds,' I said. And he laughed even louder.

'Not exactly at this moment?'

I agreed.

'What do *you* think about?'

He took his time and gave an earnest answer.

'About my son. I think about how he's got himself a good job and earns good money, I think that he's happily married and has five fine children, that he's worked his way up and is master of his own destiny, that's what I think about.'

He shot a glance up before going on, with a sigh.

'But it's not like that, he hasn't got anywhere, he's not married and has no children, and he can't do anything.'

He smiled. 'Anyway, I imagine he's happily married and has done well for himself, the way I used to think when he was a little boy and there was still hope, even though I know it's not true. It's odd, but it's nice to think about, as if it's still not too late.'

'And then I think about water,' I said, to distract him from his melancholy thoughts, and began to talk about Lake Kiantajärvi in late summer, when the water is at least twenty degrees and I can go swimming, starting off from four rocks that form steps down into the deep water, float on my back between rushes and water lilies and look at the swallows and listen to the insects humming. 'I'm a master of floating, I can even *sleep* in water.'

Antonov nodded.

'What about women?' he said dryly. 'Don't you ever think about women?'

'No,' I lied, I often thought about women, especially a teacher we had at school, Marja-Liisa Lampinen, who smelled strongly of milk at the time when my emotions were running riot, but who gradually became so skinny and frigid that now I tried to avoid her whenever we bumped into each other, I no longer delivered wood to her, I thought of her as young, it's always the young Marja-Liisa I see, while the old one can get as old as she likes, all on her own, and it struck me that I thought like Antonov, about something that no longer existed, at a time when there was still hope, as if the hope still existed, and for the first time I felt fear, as if I had received a sign that we wouldn't make it, that we had both realised this, in another moment of brotherly intimacy, not so absurd, because I could see inside this man, we were alike.

'We've got to leave,' I said. 'Wake the others. Now!'

10

Behind the house a gentle slope ran down through the spruce forest where I had hung the pig. I led the way, pulling the sled loaded with food and bedclothes and what I thought we would need in the way of equipment — axes, pots and pans, bandages, extra clothes and Rodion's shoes, too. I had fastened a rope to it, which the others had grabbed hold of or had tied around their waists. I had given Rodion the children's skis and the teacher the other pair. Behind them walked the brothers, and Mikael and Antonov brought up the rear. The strongest two ought really to have been at the front to blaze a trail, but then I would have lost contact with the weakest.

At our backs the town was in flames again, sending its red glow after us like a frozen sunset until we had passed a low knoll, and I had to decide whether to take the route along the lake, which was the simplest, or through forest and scrubland, which would be the safest.

A kilometre further north I let go of the sled and walked back along the column, looking each one of them in the eye. Neither Rodion nor Suslov met my gaze, they were breathing laboriously, neither showed any pleasure that we had managed to get through the lines safely. We had run into the frost, which hung between the tree trunks like an impenetrable wall of shattered glass.

'It's going well,' Antonov panted. 'How far have we come?'

I didn't answer, just told him to ask Mikael if he was cold. The young lad said no.

'Ask him again,' I said, 'and tell him to tell the truth.'

Mikael said no again, with irritation, but without any force.

I explained to Antonov again that if the boy got cold, he would never regain heat. The peasant asked me what the fuss was about.

'How far have we come?'

Again I did not answer.

We heard shooting ahead, towards the lake. I walked back to the sled and moved on deeper into the forest, along the timber trail I used in the summer. But we had not gone more than a few hundred metres before the teacher began to sob, and the sled became harder to pull. In the end I had to stop again. Suslov signalled that he wanted to take off his skis.

'Ask him if his legs are cold.'

The teacher said no, it was just such hard going on skis.

'It's even harder without them,' I said, and ordered him to keep them on. As far as I could see, the others were doing fine, but I still had my doubts about Mikael, who had never complained about the cold and who perhaps, for that very reason, was the most careless.

'Does he understand he has to keep moving all the time?' I asked Antonov. 'When we're standing still as well, especially his fingers and toes.'

The peasant exchanged a few words with the boy, and both said '*da*'. I took stock of the others as best I could, none of them could speak, but since I couldn't see any white patches on any of them, I decided to push on.

The teacher had stopped whimpering. But after another kilometre Rodion whispered something, then toppled over. I heard Antonov curse. The next moment Leo was lying in the snow, too, and his brother had sunk to his knees. I told Antonov to get them back up on their feet. He was rough with them, but no one shouted or said anything.

'It's no good with these weaklings,' he panted. 'We might just as well leave them behind.'

I said I had been thinking the same.

'We can't light a fire before it gets light. But if we can manage to keep moving, we should be able to get to . . .'

He snorted and turned to talk to Mikael. The boy didn't answer. For a moment, Antonov looked as if he would lose his temper.

'Let's leave the Jew and the others behind!' he snarled. 'Yes, Mikael too, he's had it, we're the only two who can make it.'

I pretended to think it over.

'We're going on,' I said. 'Do what you can to keep them on their feet.'

We crossed a number of tracks left by vehicles, skis and walkers, but followed none of them, even though that would have made the going easier. There was the odd protest from behind, but I pretended not to hear them. Then we followed another track, and soon we were standing in a pile of corpses, twenty or so Russian soldiers. Rodion screamed, the others just backed away in silence. I examined the bodies – they had all been shot, obviously trying to escape from the town, and were as stiff as boards, but why had they been left in a pile like that?

'Have they been executed?' Antonov asked.

I said I didn't think so.

'But I can't imagine who could have piled them up like this.'

In one of the kitbags I found a canteen with vodka, in another a frozen loaf, two blankets, but any weapons they might have had had been removed, and none of the clothing was of any use.

We walked on another hundred metres. I made the loggers sit on a fallen tree and asked Antonov to share out the vodka. He didn't drink any himself, just passed it on to Rodion, who immediately shouted and spat it out all over the place. Antonov managed a laugh. I said it was my fault and took the bottle from him. Then Nadar started shouting. We were sitting on another pile of corpses, which, judging by the depth of the snow, must have been lying there for close on a week. I scanned the narrow clearing and spotted several bulges under the glistening snow. Antonov kicked at the closest one, more black uniform material appeared, Russians.

'There's a boat shed a few kilometres north of town,' I said. 'We should be level with it now.'

'Have we only come *a few* kilometres?'

I ignored the question.

'It's so low that it gets completely snowed under,' I said. 'Maybe no one has found it.'

He looked imploringly at me. I said we should press on.

An hour later we found the boat shed, almost invisible beneath the snow. By then we had lost not only Rodion and Leo, but we had also returned to the war – a fierce battle was raging on the ice, just a few hundred metres away from us.

I told Antonov to dig along the inside gable wall and to chop through the bottom part of the timbers. I emptied the sled, went back and retrieved first Rodion and then Leo, who had been the first to collapse. Neither was conscious, but both were breathing.

The boat shed timbers were rotten, but coated with ice, and the peasant was exhausted when I got back. I told the loggers to lie on top of each other and fight or screw or do whatever the hell they liked so long as they kept moving, after which I set to work on the wall. The bottommost timber gave way, the next two followed.

We pulled Rodion and Leo in and laid them on the log slipway the boat had rested on. I knocked a hole in the roof and gathered all the dry twigs I could find from the nearest spruce trees. Soon we had a fire going – the smoke rose like a thin, white cord through the hole in the roof.

I told Antonov to heat the vodka and pummel the unconscious loggers, and to keep at it, even if they woke up and complained. I went out again to cut down a dead spruce tree, went back and forth with the wood, and by the time I reckoned we had enough for the next day, it was as warm in the snowed-in boat shed as it had been in Roosa and Luukas's house.

'They'll see the smoke,' Antonov said.

'Maybe. Or they'll smell it. But they have fires themselves, and we won't survive without it.'

He nodded. Then he said he could go with Nadar and get some spruce branches; I could rest.

I said I would go with them.

We collected a bundle and covered the boat-shed floor with them, put Rodion and Leo closest to the fire and wrapped them in duvets and blankets. We lay behind them, as close to each other as possible. And, one by one, we fell asleep. When I awoke, I saw that Mikael was sitting up. He had been keeping the fire going and seemed ashamed, presumably because he hadn't been helping much. I handed him the vodka canteen. He took a swallow and started to cry. I pretended not to notice and went outside – there was this greyish dawn light beneath the lustreless starry sky, the fighting on the ice had died down, but on the horizon I could make out a myriad of small, dark shapes, soldiers, horses, a scattering of smouldering, burnt-out vehicles – the final battle for Suomussalmi had been fought on ice, it looked like a rictus, there was no sign of movement.

Neither were there any footprints around the boat shed, apart from our own, and I was wondering whether I should try to cover these over when it occurred to me that if we were found, it would be Finns who found us and all they would do was take us prisoner – if they didn't shell the boat shed as soon as they spotted the smoke.

I carried more wood in, made some food and ate with Mikael. One by one the others awoke, including Rodion and Leo. Both were dazed and dizzy, but Rodion wanted his shoes back, and a quarrel broke out between the brothers. Leo said he would hate Nadar for the rest of his life for having left him in the snow.

'What life?' sneered Nadar.

Antonov laughed and translated. Even Mikael showed the last vestiges of that marten smile of his. But strangely enough none of them asked what we would do now. Nor did I make any attempt to talk about it. We were in a warm shed. We slept, we ate damp breadcrumbs, which we heated in a pan, in a paradise beneath the snow, beneath the world – we did this for a whole night and a day. But then Leo refused to go outside to piss. His brother took his side. And Antonov suggested we voted on it. I said there was no discussion, we were to shit and piss outside. Antonov had a few words with the others and said in a tone of solemn exhaustion:

'We can't take any more of this cold. I can't, either. We're not going outside.'

'Would you rather lie here and die?'

'We've already voted. There is nothing you can do about it. We're on our last legs.'

I nodded and indicated that I respected the decision. Then I said I agreed, it was a wise decision, but only on the condition that they relieved themselves in one of the pans so that I could take it outside, I also wanted their permission to collect wood for as long as I was able.

They talked among themselves for a long time before Antonov again turned to look at me.

'We have no more food,' he said. 'It takes longer to die of hunger than of cold. We can't agree.'

'What do *you* think?'

He snorted.

'I don't want you to put any more wood on the fire, it will be quicker that way, but the weaklings want you to keep the fire going, and they also want to die quickly. We've also been discussing whether you should be allowed to return to the town – you're the only one who can make it, but we can't agree on that, either.'

'Who said what?' I asked.

He was taken aback.

'I want you to go, but the others can't make up their minds.'

'Then I'll stay,' I said, and explained that I would look after the fire as I should have known we weren't strong enough, we could have stayed in Roosa and Luukas's house, and now we didn't have the strength to go back, either, I regretted it, we should never have left Suomussalmi – I hadn't done it when the fires were ravaging the houses, and I shouldn't have done it this time, either!

Antonov laid a hand on my shoulder and said not to worry.

'It's just as cold in the town,' he grinned.

Then Mikael started to babble, he was farthest away, we put him closer to the fire, but he didn't stop.

'He's talking about the cat,' Antonov said.

I told him to ask Rodion and Leo if I could examine their wounds. He told me not to bother asking. Leo had black toes on one foot, Rodion had dry, white skin from the knee down and all his fingernails were black. I rubbed them as best I could, wrapped them in bandages and went out to cut down another tree. There was still this glass wall of frozen silence everywhere, but I could see lights on the ice, from vehicles. Soon afterwards I heard sounds, too, something moving south, a convoy of horses, men, vehicles . . .

The loggers were asleep when I got back. I moved them around, got the fire going and started burning green spruce. I continued until Antonov began to cough. He woke up, looked at the smoke and went back to sleep. I put on more wood and kept this up throughout the night. Mikael awoke and seemed more clear headed, saw the smoke, but didn't say anything. I signalled that he should help me move the others. We did this without waking them, not even Antonov. They were all breathing, calmly.

I gestured to Mikael that he should go with me for more wood. That wasn't a good idea, either. He wasn't in any condition to do anything. I had to take him back, and I wasted a lot of energy.

'I'm hungry,' he gesticulated before sinking down among the others.

I went out to fetch more wood, felt something growing, both within and around me, a mighty grip which I had sensed when I had spoken to Antonov the night before we started our journey, a white expanse in a dream I understood to mean that now *I* wouldn't be able to go back, either. Nonetheless, I prepared myself. I wasn't prepared. But I was back inside before darkness fell once more.

Daylight appeared. I put more green spruce on the fire. It wasn't until much later that Antonov asked me what I was doing. I pretended not to hear, and he didn't repeat the question. I made the loggers change places, and said that Suslov should tell us a story – he hadn't said a word since we arrived at the boat shed, and he wasn't speaking now either, not even when Antonov began to kick him.

'I didn't know it hurt so much to freeze to death,' Leo said.

Antonov said it wasn't the cold, it was the hunger. And the

quarrel flared up again, but it was half-hearted and broken by long pauses – meanwhile I kept adding more spruce to the fire.

At around midnight I heard sounds, it must have been midnight, I crawled out and saw lights on the ice again, vehicles moving south.

I crept back in and put the biggest logs on the fire, and on top of them another pile of spruce, the flames shot up all along the gable wall, the beams in the roof caught fire, and the loggers awoke one after the other, coughing, although only the brothers showed any sign of panic. Antonov again asked what I was up to, Suslov and Mikael said nothing.

The whole west wall caught fire, and the roof started to drip. We retreated from the flames and the dripping water and squeezed up against the remaining wall.

'At least it will be quick now,' Antonov said.

Because of the melting ice the fire was burning more sluggishly, but the smoke was getting thicker. Then the timbers dried, and eventually the roof also caught fire, the whole roof, we had to get out. I wondered whether I had committed another folly. The loggers stared with lifeless eyes. I said we should lie down on what was left of the spruce branches, as close to the burning boat shed as we could, gradually moving closer as it burnt down.

'After that it will be quick,' I said.

Again they did as I asked.

*

I was woken by a low buzz of voices, I wanted to see my forests in front of my eyes, trees dancing in warm summer winds, but a stabbing pain shot up through my foot. At my side I saw Mikael's mouth and a swollen tongue uttering a silent prayer. Around us in the luminous blue morning light stood a dozen white-clad figures, all of them with weapons slung over their shoulders. On the ice, close to the shore, was a truck with its engine running, shrouded in its own white exhaust fumes.

I sat up and saw the loggers lying in a semicircle around a black sun in the snow. It was cold. It was desperately cold. One of the soldiers approached, the snow scrunching under his boots, and said something in Finnish. I said something, too.

'Finnish? Are you Finnish?'

'I'm the logger here,' I said.

He smiled into his frozen beard.

'I can see that. Can you get up?'

I couldn't. My foot was frozen solid in something black that had once been water. 'Who are they?' he asked, nodding towards the others.

'They're loggers, like me.'

I I

One of the best things I know is to wake up slowly in a bed I don't need to leave. Then I think about trees, the trees I have felled and the trees I will fell, if I'm lucky, all the trunks I've blazed, standing there, gleaming and filling me with excitement and expectation. But, above all, I'm overwhelmed by all the trees I *won't* fell, the ones I leave, all the ones I won't have time to do, the forest as it is, spreading out in all directions, where I run about like a confused animal, unable to find my way out, it's like standing before a locked door and not being able to find your name — then I wake up in a sweat, choking, and have to see the sky so that I can breathe. But now it is the sound of chains which wakes me, the iron caterpillar tracks and the roar of engines, but no shouts, no shots either, and the man sitting at my bedside on a folding chair and chain-smoking, I've seen him before, he is writing something on a scrap of paper; he looks at it with displeasure and sees I am awake, he crumples it up and puts it in his pocket.

'Ah,' he says. 'There you are.'

'What's on the paper?' I ask, my tongue sticking to my teeth.

'Nothing,' he snaps, and flicks up another cigarette. 'Do you recognise me?'

I recognise him. He doesn't seem quite so drained any more, but the restless unease is there, like insects beneath the skin, it's Olli, the lieutenant in charge of setting fire to the town. I am lying on a field stretcher resting on packed, dry ground, in a tent with blackened stovepipes stretching like columns up through the canvas billowing above a small armada of beds and men and nurses. It smells of Finland – Finnish smoke, Finnish diesel, soap, cigarette smoke, oil, food . . . And I am wearing dry, freshly washed Finnish clothes.

'Where am I?'

'In Suomussalmi. You'll be questioned as soon as you're well. But I think it's best if we . . . I thought I'd never see you again, I have to admit.'

'Questioned?'

He peers at me, with indifference.

'I don't know, I suppose they'll want to know why the Russians didn't kill you.'

'I wasn't a threat to them.'

'Then perhaps they'll be interested to know whether you were of any *help* to them.'

He lets that sink in and then continues.

'Yes, and I think it's best if we have a chat first. You tell me what you've been doing here these last few weeks, up north in Kiantajärvi with the Russian soldiers. Cigarette?'

I say no and close my eyes.

'They're not soldiers,' I say. But he doesn't react to that, he smokes. 'How are my feet?' I ask, because I can't feel them.

'They had to take two toes off the left foot, but you won't even notice. Your Russian friends are alive too, but none of them will talk, and that's stupid of them. I hope it was hell there.'

I open my eyes.

'Have you got a mirror?'

He seems to have been waiting for the question. I have a pocket mirror held up in front of my face and see that two irregular cuts along my left cheek have been sewn with stitches looking like black ants, my nose is still crooked, blue and swollen, and the cut to my upper lip is held together by something resembling safety pins. I run my fingertips along the column of ants.

'Pretty face.' Olli smiles. 'Smashed nose, smashed cheekbone. Beaten up?'

'Yes.'

'Why?'

'Because I . . .'

I hesitate. I have always hesitated in situations like this, and say something different to the first thing that comes into my head. 'Because I didn't want to cooperate.'

'What did you do, then?'

'I chopped wood.'

He rolls his eyes.

'The country is in its worst ever crisis, and you chop wood, for the *enemy*?'

'I had no choice.'

'I see. And where did you live? Were you a prisoner . . .?'

I say the second thing that comes into my head and sound more exhausted than I am, and when I finally finish, or pretend to be on the point of passing out, he stubs out his cigarette and says 'I see' a couple of times and mumbles, for fear of flapping ears in neighbouring beds:

'I think I would drop the bit about translating messages for them, the whole division's dead and can't tell any tales . . . Are you sure you won't have a cigarette?'

Now from behind closed eyes again I say no and hear him getting up and walking around in his squeaky boots before leaving. But when I think no one's looking and I open my eyes to take a cautious peep, he is still there, with a smug grin because he has caught me out.

'Water!' I cry out in panic, and there's a bit of toing and froing until an orderly appears with water and asks how I feel, and I have to drink more than I need before Olli finally reveals what is on his mind:

'You stayed behind *voluntarily*, do we agree on that?'

I nod.

'Nothing can remove me from here. Not even you.'

I try to smile. He deliberates, lights another cigarette and leaves.

The day after I am already back on my feet, with a full stomach, rested and warm, my face still hurting, but the wounds are cleaned and the dressings changed every morning and night, and the two small toes on my left foot really don't make any difference one way or the other, it is more a question of why I was ever born with them in the first place.

I walk around in new boots, in new, warm clothes. But I don't go far. I walk around inside the tent, and talk to the wounded, soldiers suffering from frostbite and bullet wounds, who moan in their sleep and when awake, and want painkillers, cigarettes, spirits . . . I hear about battles and battalions, men and regiments, heroes, victories and catastrophes.

But there is no sign of the men I am looking for, the loggers, and no one can tell me anything about them, either – so I sleep through more short dreams until the third day, when I venture outside into the bitter cold, and I can sense with a melancholy shiver that quiet reigns in the ruins of a town where everything that had already been comprehensively destroyed has been destroyed a second time. There are soldiers and vehicles, white-clad Finnish men, and the same everyday sounds of engines that hummed with such pleasant restraint before the flames devoured everything. Not even on the horizon is there any sign of the war, it has been pushed farther east, four, five, six kilometres, to where the Russian reinforcements are still stuck and fighting, a snake, tens of kilometres long from the Soviet Union, reaching into the belly of Finland, a corridor of iron, logs and ice, unable to turn, unable to retreat, so it has no choice but to wait to be sliced into pieces and perish in the same systematic way that Illyushin's forces were destroyed on the ice of Lake Kiantajärvi, this lake of death that will forever be haunted by a silence only found in cemeteries without crosses, my lake, which I can look across from where I am standing outside this heavenly tent and which has been scored in all directions by vehicle tracks and looks like a black grid, and it's then I feel a void inside, I have to go back, back to bed and sleep.

*

But as the days pass, my walks become longer, I can inspect Antti's shop, which is still in one piece but occupied by Finnish soldiers, whom I greet and ask to take good care of the building, and Babushka's newly cleaned house, which serves as a headquarters and mess hall, steam pouring out of its doors and windows dispersing the aroma of freshly baked bread, birch wood and the meat broth I have eaten ever since I was born, and it smells better than Marja-Liisa Lampinen's pungent milk.

No one is interested in my Russian friends. I hear about a prison camp in Hulkonniemi, but I can't walk there yet, and there's a limit to how much I can dig or delve – but on my way back to the tent, I spot a man I never thought I would ever see again, Nikolai, the interpreter, engaged in a conversation with a *Finnish* officer, and he looks the way he did before his Russian hopes disintegrated, as if he belongs here too, although he doesn't. And I make up my mind to avoid him.

It doesn't work. We bump into each other again the very next day, and it's then that I discover it is Nikolai who wants to avoid *me*, and it feels as it did when we sat opposite each other before the collapse; we walk round each other, looking the other way, it's a strategy we share, our tacit agreement, him in conversation with a Finnish officer, me trudging my way towards Roosa and Luukas's house, where I have wanted to go for a long time, but have lacked the strength. It is depressing to discover that the north wall has taken a direct hit, into the kitchen – it must have happened only hours after we left.

I go inside and take hold of the water pump and realise it won't budge, not a single cup in the cupboard is in one piece, not a plate, not a chair, the wall-clock hangs at a slant, the glass shattered, and the hour-hand points between two and three. I look for Mikke, and can't find him, and that makes the house feel even more devastated.

I walk around the other rooms, and the beds are as we left them, and I have to admit they are in a dreadful state. I have now reached the point where I can't even remember what we were thinking when we ran off, believing we would survive. I have to sit down. I sit on Roosa and Luukas's double bed, where Mikael and Suslov slept, and notice Roosa's glasses case on the bedside table. My hands pick it up and open it, and inside I find the glasses and a little note with a few almost illegible Russian words, but I recognise the word for 'thank you' and the name Alexander Suslov, and then I cannot get up again, I fall back against the dirty pillows and pull the freezing cold duvet, without its cover, over me, and smell something that makes me wonder why we never realise the wretched state we are in while we are in it – you think you're alive, even when half dead. I have gone from being the strongest to being so weak that I can barely drag myself the few hundred metres from the field hospital to where I am now lying with closed eyes, holding a glasses case, this small object that is the final blow, but it is a necessary part of the process, although it takes time – I think it is the dreams which take time.

When, finally, I can stand up again, I am warm, and as I go back into the kitchen I no longer think the damage is that serious – a new wall is needed, only splinters remain of the wood panelling, and the doors have no panels, swinging frames on torn-off hinges, benches and tables need repairing, new glass for the windows, and shrapnel growing out of the floorboards like a thick metal lawn.

I find a pair of pliers in the scrapheap outside and start pulling the shrapnel out, tidy up and throw away everything that cannot be repaired, including the chair I spent so many hours in, and I think there is already an improvement, almost like the beginning of a new life.

The other rooms are less damaged, the roof is intact, everywhere in the house, and the stoves, too. And before I leave I also take a hammer head from the scrapheap and nail up the front door as my mind begins to hatch a plan, I don't think I have lived a single day without having some kind of plan in mind. When you are awake you have to have a plan. Once again I will have to find a way of fitting the insufferable interpreter into it.

I 2

There was talk of evacuating the wounded as soon as the road west had been secured, if there were enough vehicles, there was a regular shuttle service all along the chaotic front — this was going through my mind as I lay in bed, and sleep would not come, so in the small hours of the night I got up again, packed a bag of clothes, crept out, and long before daybreak I was busy ripping materials off Luukas's half-burnt barn — planks and bits of board, and also quite a few pieces of planed panelling he had used to line his cow stalls. Using the broken tools, I set to work on the outer wall around the kitchen. And, as before, no one reacted. But at around noon I felt hungry and went back to the field hospital, and there some people did react. I calmed them down by assuring them I was in good shape, which the nurses strongly disagreed with, but I was given all the food I wanted, ate it slowly, in the Russian manner, had my wounds redressed, and pretended not to hear when the nurses wanted me back in bed.

By evening I had sealed the whole of the outer wall and was well on my way with the inside panelling. There were a good many problems, scores of joints and lots of patching, it wasn't what you would call neat workmanship.

But at around midnight I was stoking the stove when I noticed that smoke was seeping out through a crack in the chimney. I was going to the barn to get a bucket of tar when they came for me, an armed soldier and the nurse who had earlier dressed my wounds.

I had to go back with them to the field hospital, had to get into bed too, and was annoyed when the soldier drew up a chair and sat down by my side, the rifle across his knees. He couldn't have been more than twenty years old, but had already adopted that fixed expression I had seen on the faces of so many soldiers. I asked him his name and where he was from. He hardly bothered to answer, was more preoccupied with sitting still as instructed and keeping watch over this object that didn't interest him in the slightest. Things were beginning to return to the way they once were here.

I lay for a while trying to devise a plan of escape, but it was warm under the blankets, no one was screaming any more, everyone was sleeping in the beds around me, peace, and soon I was asleep, too.

When I opened my eyes, Olli was standing there.

'We're leaving,' he said with a contented grin, smoke billowing out of both nostrils.

'I'm staying,' I said. 'I have been given permission to stay.'

His grin broadened.

'By whom?'

'Lieutenant Colonel Mäkiniemi,' I said, a name that had caught my ear over the last few days, a hero, as far as I could understand, whose words ought to carry some weight.

But Olli didn't even bother to comment.

'Can you sit up?' he asked.

'I can walk,' I said. 'I can run.'

'Good,' he said. 'Then you can come with me. Get your clothes on. This minute!'

I did as he ordered, put on all the outdoor clothing they had laid out for me, and, accompanied by the soldier, walked out to the waiting vehicle, an open jeep. But to my surprise, Olli himself was behind the wheel and he told me to sit in the seat beside him.

'Wasn't I supposed to be interrogated?' I asked.

'No,' he said, seeming to bite back a 'fortunately'. 'Now jump in.'

'I am not leaving Suomussalmi,' I said, and stood my ground. 'I have said it before and I will say it again.'

'Come on,' Olli said humourlessly. 'Unless you want to be packed off with the prisoners?'

I got in.

There was a lot of traffic, it was slow going, and as we passed a command centre set up close to where the Russians had had theirs, I spotted a group of officers drinking coffee outside a field kitchen. I jumped out, ran off and placed myself squarely in front of the man I considered the highest-ranking officer, and attempted a military salute. Only then did I see that he was a colonel, and not just any colonel either, I was to learn later, but Colonel Hjalmar Siilasvuo, the commanding officer of the most successful front division in Finland's thousand-year history.

'I beg the colonel's permission to stay in Suomussalmi,' I bellowed. 'I am from here and I am not leaving.'

Long experience of people worthier than me has taught me that if you have something to say, then look them straight in the eye and say it – a couple of times, if necessary – and continue to look at them, then as a rule they will listen. 'I am a logger,' I went on, 'I chop wood – and your detachments need wood, a lot of wood.'

There was a deathly silence around us. All eyes were fixed on me, including Olli's. He had parked the jeep and was now standing next to me, nervously shuffling his feet, but I had eyes only for the colonel.

'*Wood* . . . ?' he announced in a faraway voice, as though talking of ghosts.

'Yes, *wood*,' I said. 'Without wood not even the colonel can win this war. And I can supply several cords a day, split and ready for use. If I have a free hand, I can also undertake to . . .'

He stopped me with a tiny flick of his hand.

'What happened to your face?'

'I was a prisoner and was beaten up, by a Russian officer.'

'Why?'

'He didn't like my face.'

I suspect this must have been the only time in the whole campaign that the colonel permitted himself a smile, but it was meagre and thin and seemed to give him more pain than pleasure. A staff officer leaned over and whispered something in his ear. Siilasvuo nodded imperceptibly, cast another glance in my direction and, without another word, turned his back on me in order to resume the conversation I had interrupted.

I stood there looking in bewilderment from Olli to the staff officer. Both shrugged, uncertain but not unsympathetic, as far as I could judge, and as Olli lit up another

cigarette, I thought I detected in his face the trace of resig-
nation I was after.

'Do you have anywhere to live?' he asked as we walked
back to the jeep. 'You can't stay in the field hospital any
longer. You're well enough . . .'

'Yes,' I said.

He stopped and pulled a slip of paper from his breast
pocket, wrote something on it with the stub of a pencil and
handed it to me.

'Give this man my regards and tell him to put you to
work, and to give you the toughest jobs you can possibly
manage. And do as I tell you for once, otherwise nothing
will ever get sorted out around here.'

'Like when the town was burned down,' I said, limping
off in the direction he indicated before he had time to
change his mind, towards a depot that was being built in the
eastern part of town. There I reported to Harri Miettinen,
a sullen, large, swarthy bear of a reserve officer who had
been told he was useless at the front and had therefore been
assigned the job of supplying the field hospital, the military
headquarters and a unit of guards with food and equipment
– and also wood, a task he decided to perform just as
effectively as Colonel Siilasvuo had in conducting the war.

As soon as I asked to be given the hardest work I could
cope with, we became good friends, and even better friends
when on the very first evening he was able to verify that I did

the work of two of the other loggers he had working for him, out of whom he did his utmost to squeeze the last drop. 'This is no holiday camp, the war isn't over yet, there's a whole armoured division out there, waiting to be cleaned up . . .'

Here in Suomussalmi it was not even breathed as a possibility that the Russians might be able to reverse the catastrophic turn of events, which they seemed to be doing on the Karelian isthmus, we were in the burnt-out town of miracles, my town.

'Watch the idiot,' Harri Miettinen would roar, pointing at me. 'Watch and learn!'

13

I thought now I had recovered most of the strength I had once had. And after just a couple of days, Miettinen lost interest in me, at least he didn't care what I did in the hours he presumed I was asleep.

First of all, I sealed the crack in the chimney with the help of fragments of broken cups, clay and tar, and fired up both stoves, then I went on to repair the interior, and only a few hours later the water pipe started to gurgle. I forged a new handle for the water pump, hammered the dents out of two pots and started on the sitting room and the bedrooms, after that I washed the bedclothes, and hung them up to dry in the kitchen, so that I could wander back and forth with the long-handled broom between clean-smelling white sheets, humming like a priest or a farmer's wife or whoever hums when they work, watchmakers perhaps, people with quiet, precise professions. I went about my jobs in the sitting room and on the stairs and kept going until the sheets were dry before crawling into what must have been the warmest and cleanest of all the beds to be found that night along the whole front, Markku's bed, Markku, who, just over a month ago, had died fighting on the isthmus.

The next day I told Miettinen to his face that I had a house in town and asked whether he had anything against my living there. He said no. And I don't know what the reason was, but it was as easy as that, I had enough food, enough clothes for my needs, my wounds were as good as healed. Among the shrapnel on the kitchen floor I had found the minute-hand of the clock; now I fixed it back on with a piece of copper wire and set it to twelve, as I thought it had to be around midnight. The day after, I discovered it was half an hour fast and I wound it back, so that was that done, and now not even I thought the Russians would gain any more from their adventure than their own destruction.

I moved two doors from the outhouse and hung them in the hall, replaced a few of the floorboards in the kitchen and repaired the cupboards – they looked fine, but the walls were a sorry sight, and I had already rejected the idea of ripping out panels from one of the other surviving houses.

As the days went by, however, it irritated me more and more to see Roosa and Luukas's beautiful house disembowelled and half dead. I needed some windowpanes, as dark boards were still where the kitchen windows had been, sealed with rags and tar, but where do you find unbroken glass in a town that has been razed to the ground?

I started by taking six small panes from the peepholes at the back of the outhouse. Then I worked loose the two remaining panes in the window in what was left of a foundation wall, these wouldn't be of any use to anyone, I reckoned. I whittled some new bars and uprights, nailed them to the frames and held the panes in place with tacks and tar, I didn't have any putty, but now at least I had daylight, for as long as it lasted, and that evening I sat in the kitchen drinking coffee, watching, through the new glass, snow falling like dry sand, half a window with eight small panes as polished and clear as daylight itself – I thought about the loggers and something Antonov had asked me before we lost touch.

'Why are you doing this for us?'

I had been waiting for the question and also looked forward to it in a way, as I had planned to answer that I had done nothing special, but when it came I no longer knew, so I didn't answer, or else I passed out.

I went outside and looked at the new snow, which reminded me of icing sugar on top of all the blackness.

I expected to see something. I did, too, I saw paw marks and followed them around the house and found Mikke coiled up on top of the woodpile, licking his paws, the snow glistening in his grey fur, he stiffened and looked straight at me with narrowed eyes, jumped down and followed me inside. I gave him some leftovers and a drop of milk, sat down in the chair by the stove to watch while he ate his fill. Then he jumped up on my lap, made himself comfortable and started to purr.

The moon hung in the sky like the bottom of a well. And I walked beneath it, through my frozen town, thinking again about the Russian loggers and asking myself whether they had ever existed, whether anything at all had ever existed, when I suddenly noticed a truck parked outside one of the houses where Nikolai, the interpreter, had lit fires during the days before the town fell. Three old men in civilian clothes were sitting on the doorstep smoking, while a fourth dragged a box towards the door. I stopped and stood watching – civilian men. Now I also thought I recognised the first and the second, they were from Suomussalmi, so I went a few steps closer and said hello and asked what they were doing there.

'The logger,' said one of them, immediately putting on the sneer you could see everywhere here before the war.

'We live here,' the second said.

'You've come back, then?' I asked.

'Yes,' said a long, curved figure with a marsh-brown beard and white hair. He got to his feet, a spokesman for the others, and sized me up with bright, blinking, runny eyes. 'And you?'

It sounded almost threatening.

'I've been here all the time.'

They found that amusing.

I told them where I was living and pointed to Roosa and Luukas's house. And the man with the beard nodded towards the ruins next to him and said that had been his friend's home, and it would be again, the four of them were neighbours who had managed to trick their way through the barriers in the west of the town because now they were sick and tired of this war, they regretted they had ever left their homes and had not stayed to defend them.

'That might not have been so easy,' I said. And that did not seem to amuse them.

'So you've been here all the time?' said the man with the marsh-brown beard and the runny eyes.

'Yes,' I repeated.

They glanced at each other and smiled again, this sneer I knew so well and had not missed for a single moment since it had disappeared.

'I hope you gave the Russians a nice reception, ha ha . . .'

Another leaden weight sank in my insides.

'I borrowed your clock,' I said to put an end to this, and turned towards the man with the box. 'If you want it back, I can go and get it right away.'

There was this indefinable tingling of the blood that you get when you feel you are being observed.

'A clock?' he said slowly.

I walked ahead of him into the house, his own house, which had been wrecked beyond recognition by soldiers who had obviously slept in the kitchen and in the sitting room – the floors were covered with torn, filthy bed-clothes, stiff with cold, the tap had sprung a leak, and the leaking water had frozen to enclose the sink and half the worktop in a green glass dome, from which two greedy tongues stretched towards the back door and the cellar trapdoor, cupboard doors and wall coverings had been ripped off for use as firewood, cups and glasses had been smashed, the stove had been knocked to pieces, and the sitting room was just as bad.

'There,' I said, pointing to the wall above what looked like a rotting animal, a sofa, and the old man stood next to me with tears in his eyes staring at what can happen to a home left to the dictates of a war. 'There was a clock there,' I said. 'I've looked after it. Do you want it back?'

Now, at least, he managed to restrain this laugh I had never missed.

'Oh yes, the clock,' he mumbled. 'It's old.'

'I'll go and get it at once,' I said, and walked back to Luukas and Roosa's house, took the clock off a wall where it had been at home for a good month, and took it to the wall where it had ticked away for perhaps fifty or a hundred years, and where it would certainly have been destroyed if *I* had not taken care of it.

The old men stood staring at me in amazement.

'Did you steal it?' exclaimed the man with the beard, the spokesman, who was the most stupid of them and therefore said aloud what the others were content to think.

'No,' I said, hanging the clock on the hook. 'I needed a clock and borrowed it. Now it's back in its place again.'

Before they had a chance to brood on their dark suspicions, I left them and went home and didn't sleep, the next morning I went to the depot to ask Miettinen to billet me with the others, I couldn't stay in Roosa and Luukas's house any longer. Why not? Because four old men had returned and had found their homes in ruins, four old men who at first refused to believe that I had been there all the time, but who then were more than willing to believe I had used the opportunity to rob them while they were away, it was like something that had always been here and I had never liked, these accusations that confront each other but still refuse to go away, a darkness some of us are enveloped in from the day we are born and never learn to see through, we look through water with our own eyes, for it was while I was standing like a sinner before Miettinen that

I finally realised why I had not allowed myself to be evacuated by Olli and his soldiers, I had done no more than what was expected of me, I had been who I am, the one who stays behind when everyone else leaves, ordered around by an old codger with a marsh-brown beard and his neighbours. It was this darkness I had never been able to see through before, and now the light was of no help either, because what kind of peace would this be, if it was no more than a repeat of the previous one?

But at the depot another surprise was awaiting me, four Russian prisoners, among them my friend Antonov, the stocky little peasant from Kalevala in Russian Karelia, dressed in new Finnish clothes and boots, holding an axe in one hand and a wedge in the other, hands well hidden in mittens the size of skinned bears, and a smile so distant that it could only mean that we should not acknowledge each other's presence while Miettinen was watching. So I turned to the depot manager and asked:

'Who are these people?'

'Russians, we're getting more tomorrow. You can drive them as hard as you like, they look robust enough.'

'Prisoners of war aren't supposed to work,' I said.

'Really?' Miettinen said, surprised. 'Ask them.'

I was about to say something, but the depot manager got in first, turning to Antonov and yelling in Finnish:

'You want to work?'

Antonov acted as if it was only now he understood what was going on, and answered with a few vigorous nods.

'Happy?' Miettinen said to me, and there was no reason for me not to be, of course. But now at least it had been said, that I knew that prisoners of war weren't supposed to work, unless forced to by someone committing an injustice.

The work was the same, but it still felt quite different, we weren't shot at, we could move freely over larger areas, fell the trees at our own pace and have horses pull them out safely over snow-covered log trails, as horses should.

Antonov had no problems keeping up with us, although his fellow-prisoners found it a hard grind. But the whole of this first day was to pass before we contrived to have time alone together − after the onset of night − and could give each other a hug, again he called me his angel, his life and hope, and would not let me go until I pushed him away. His language was just as unclear as when we first met. But his Finnish words gradually came back to life, and he told me that the other loggers had survived as well. It had been hardest for the brothers, who had had several toes and fingers amputated and had been put to work only a couple of days ago; Rodion had been adopted by the troops who had found us, they thought it was funny with those shoes he carried around with him, and had taken him with them to the front, as a mascot − he made coffee for them and cooked their meals, pulled a little sledge loaded with provisions and ammunition, he also had enough clothes and food.

'And Mikael?'

Mikael had refused to talk for more than a week, and after that had only grinned and babbled something that was neither Finnish nor Russian, they thought he had gone mad. But then, all of a sudden, he was his old self again, since even the longest night has to turn in to day at some point, now he was putting in fence posts around the camp in Hulkonniemi.

'And the teacher? Is he still blind?'

'Yes, and because he's no use to anyone, he still feels cold, even though he's allowed to stay in a tent and has enough clothing.'

I considered this.

'Tell him he should ask the guards to be allowed to work with you. He should say he can chop wood and that's all he's ever done – he's a logger.'

Antonov nodded seriously and appeared to give this some thought. But his mind was elsewhere.

'There's something I have to tell you,' he said, then closed his mouth, unable to go on.

'Yes?' I said.

'I want to say thank you,' he said with earnestness, after which he drew his right hand out of the bear-glove and held it out to me, and as we shook hands and looked at each other, I knew that from now on this man would be willing to die for me, as no one had ever been before, with the possible exception of my parents, but I could no longer remember any of that and oddly enough, this was such a huge change between us, it was almost impossible to bear, I could see into him, we were now one person, I didn't even think of him as Russian and of myself as Finnish, or that this was not peace, but war, as I ought to have done.

Miettinen shouted that work was over for the day, Antonov and the others were collected by a guard and taken back to the prison camp, I walked with the depot manager and told him I wanted to live in town after all, unless he objected. He looked at me and said he didn't mind what I did, as long as I did what was asked of me. I thanked him, was given another sceptical glance and went home via the log-floaters' cottage, where I had found coffee when the town was burning. Here I found some cups and six plates, took six small panes from the cellar window and did not feel the least shame.

On passing the old school grounds I saw a yellow flicker behind the iced-up windows in the 'clock-house', smoke was rising from the chimney, and it struck me that I should go in there one final time, I had no plan, it was simply the kind of impulse you have when an indefinable smile radiates to every part of your body, the reunion with Antonov had brought this about, had given me the strength.

I knocked on the door, walked in and saw the old men sitting in the kitchen drinking from small glasses they had placed on the red-hot stove. The water pipe had been repaired, the enormous lump of ice had been transformed into a wet, newly washed floor.

I realised I had nothing to say, so I stood there for a while before asking if they had enough wood. Yes, they did, was there anything else? And I suppose *that* was the answer I had been expecting. Because now I remembered the man with the marsh-brown beard, he had bought wood from me a few times, and he was the type who took an eternity to pay, who dragged the purse out of his pocket as if it weighed more than one man had the strength to lift, who took out the coins and notes, weighed them lingeringly, probably in both hands, put them back and pulled them out again before finally parting with them, with an expression that said he had been cheated. He was a skinflint.

'I recognise you now,' I said. 'You owe me money.'

'What?'

'I delivered logs to you last winter, and you never paid me.'

I stood my ground. And as he didn't answer, the others turned to look at him, first expectantly, then for a moment almost as if they were on my side. And when I knew that he couldn't sit there any longer without answering, I broke the silence and said there was no rush and went home to the cat and sat in the kitchen wondering how I could find more glass for the windows. I have that strength of mind, if there is something I don't want to think about, I don't.

The next morning we were already well into our work when the guards came with the Russian prisoners, and among them now was not only Antonov, but also Mikael, Suslov, the teacher, and the brothers from Kiev. Mikael was just as moved as Antonov to see me. Suslov cried when he heard my voice, twisted his head in my direction, and cried even more when I was able to slip him Roosa's glasses while the guards weren't looking. He immediately put them on with what seemed like demented exultation.

For their part, Nadar and Leo seemed embarrassed and insecure, and even when the three of us were alone together acted as if they had met a relative they had cheated out of money when their paths last crossed. But before we could exchange more than a few words, Miettinen came swaggering along wanting to send the brothers back to the camp, as they were limping worse than ever now because of their amputated toes.

I felt like saying they could work like few others, which was true, but they themselves protested so violently that Miettinen asked Antonov what all the shouting was about.

The peasant explained that the two brothers were as strong as bears and would simply go to pieces if not given something to do. The depot manager growled sullenly that they were Antonov's responsibility in that case. He said the cripples had this one day to show what they could do, this wasn't a holiday camp, the war wasn't over, it had only just begun . . .

There were now so many of us that we were split into two groups. I was given the task of leading one, consisting of the old loggers plus a middle-aged Finn I had become good friends with. His name was Heikki and he had a farm near the border, a property he had evacuated and now suspected was in the Russians' filthy hands.

'I don't like the Russians,' he would say, and by and large that was all he ever said. But he regarded the prisoners in the same way as he did everyone else, as if they didn't exist. Since his wife died and his kids moved out, Heikki had lived on his own, and that seemed to have been for most of his life. He was small, stocky and tough, a horse breeder who had his own farm and had grafted all his life.

We had barely started on this blue-cold January morning before Nadar and Leo manoeuvred their way over to join Antonov and me and started apologising for having messed up our escape.

I assured them that the blunder was not their fault, it was mine alone, I knew what cold temperatures were, they didn't, we should never have left the house. But Antonov strongly disagreed with this; he screamed something at them and could not be bothered to translate their responses.

'Idiots,' he mumbled. 'Jews.'

I soon got them back to work.

But this day and this work, so far from the front that we could hardly hear it, gradually became so like an ordinary working day in these parts that I forgot the whole business, only occasionally stopping to listen and look around – at Suslov and Mikael, who, oblivious, ploughed their way through the snow and the mass of branches, at Heikki, who kept the horses in check with bad-tempered snorts and little growling noises. We cut dry spruce the frost had not got into, and waded through the yellow-white sawdust that looked like pulverised beeswax, with the sounds of two axes trying to outdo each other, the dull song of saw blades, the dry, ripping groans of logs being cloven and with the smoke from the fire we ate around shimmering like water . . . But then it struck me that even though everything was now as it should be, that was exactly what it wasn't, something had been taken away, by a powerful hand, a wall was missing, the most gruesome mutilation was taking place just a few kilometres away, and we didn't hear it, we took a deep breath and held it – and so the days passed, undisturbed, alongside this missing wall, as cold and clear as drops of silence, a slow train through time that would have come to a complete standstill, had it not been for Miettinen's short, sporadic outbursts, Heikki's wordless conversations with the horses, hot food, rough hands no longer frozen, the smell of resin and smoke, bodies growing stronger and stronger, one week, two weeks, then another week . . .

All this time the brothers from Kiev kept on about something the other Russians wouldn't discuss, and Antonov refused to explain. Until one evening around the fire Suslov told a story that made the others laugh, Antonov too. And during the hullabaloo, the peasant leant over to me and whispered that the brothers wanted to talk to me.

'What about?' I asked.

He looked at Heikki, who was sitting staring into the flames and thinking about his farmstead. I told Antonov to speak openly.

'We've heard we're going to be sent back home, in exchange for Finnish prisoners.'

'Yes?'

'But they say we'll be shot when we get back.'

'Just what you deserve.' Heikki laughed out loud, displaying a great, toothless cavity none of us had seen before. Antonov managed to keep his composure. 'You're animals,' Heikki continued, as if talking to himself. And still Antonov didn't react. 'But there are good animals too. The horses here, for instance, they're good animals, and I think you could be too, yes, hm, hm.' He nodded. 'Damn you.'

'I don't believe a word of it . . .' I said.

'But that's what these idiots are going around saying. And I . . . I want to go home, so long as I am not killed. I can't live here, I hate this country, this war, the Finns, the cold weather . . .'

Heikki looked at Antonov, clapped his mittens together and smiled. For a brief moment it looked as if the Russian might lose his temper.

'I think you should go home,' I said.

But there was something wrong in these days that followed each other so dependably, the missing wall, the brothers' discussion, so I took them aside and told them, with Antonov's ill-tempered help, that they should stop this talk, it was dangerous, for all of us, it was also a terrible lie.

They wanted to protest. But we didn't give them the opportunity. Besides, there was something I had to look into before I could change another plan I had been mulling over during this time when everything was harmonious and yet was not.

Every morning Miettinen consulted Heikki and me about the day's work, though always in the form of shouted orders, and the day after the discussion around the fire I chose a section of forest a good kilometre north of town, a large area to log, and then told Miettinen we needed skis.

'Can't you find some trees closer to town?'

'We still need skis.'

Heikki was standing next to me and said he wouldn't mind a pair of skis, either.

'We haven't even enough skis for the soldiers.'

'What about those?'

Heikki nodded towards one of the sheds in Miettinen's charge, filled with the surplus equipment civilians had collected.

In a few hours we each had skis, or as good as, with poles, bindings and boots that fitted, more or less. And now I spent all the time I could find teaching the brothers and Suslov how to use them. Antonov and Mikael already knew how to ski. And Heikki pretended not to notice what was going on.

I loaded a sled with wood and harnessed one of the horses, and every day for the next few days I did a round in Suomussalmi as if I were the logger calling on customers. I kept a lookout for Nikolai, the traitor and interpreter, he was never on his own and seemed to be sticking to his policy of not recognising me. But I am the type who does not give up easily, and one afternoon I headed straight for him, quickly jumped off the sled and stood in his path, he was with a Finnish non-commissioned officer, whom I ignored when I asked Nikolai where he wanted the wood.

'*The wood?*'

'You asked me to get you a load of wood. Where do you want it?'

Something must have told him that I was capable of exploiting this delivery to the utmost, so he mouthed a vague 'yes' while his eyes scanned the ruins and settled on staff quarters on the slope leading to the bay on the northern side of the headland.

'I think it's down there,' he mumbled. 'I'll show you.'

We left the Finn and went on foot, me with the reins over my shoulder so the horse's head bobbed up and down between us.

Nikolai snarled:

'What the hell do you want now?'

I said we should walk down to the quarters so that we could talk undisturbed while I unloaded the wood.

'Some of the prisoners in Hulkonniemi have been assigned to cut wood,' I said when we got there. 'The same men who did the job when the Russians were here. I want you to tell the Finns they're not soldiers and never have been. They're civilians who were forced into this war against their will.'

'Why should I do that?' Nikolai said, now the trader who has spotted his chance to barter. I ignored him.

'You can wait for an opportunity,' I continued, 'and sooner or later you'll get one, and then you'll tell them that those six loggers have never worn a uniform.'

'I could tell them you collaborated with us.'

I smiled.

'Cutting wood?'

'Exactly,' he said, and again it was how it had always been between us, we were both so guilty there was nothing to be said. Even so, he asked me if I was threatening him.

'I'm asking you to tell the truth about these Russians,' I insisted. 'Your own countrymen.'

Even though he stood there just as he had done when he hadn't been able to make up his mind whether to kill me or use me, I knew that the conversation ought to finish before one of us got any bright ideas into our heads, so I quickly said that the staff here were not getting any more wood, climbed on to the sled and drove back to the loggers.

Three days later I told Miettinen that Heikki and I were sleeping in Roosa and Luukas's house, I said it was a big house and there was enough room for the rest of the loggers, too, so they wouldn't have to provide transport every day.

To my surprise he said he had been thinking along the same lines, but he thought it was too risky, the prisoners might try to escape, although there was nowhere to escape to, but then the Russians are not like other people, and then we would be left without any loggers.

I knew he didn't want to admit that he had already aired the idea with a superior officer and had been told no.

'Oh well,' I said. 'The house is there, anyway.'

Two days later the convoy of prisoners was escorted by a single jeep occupied by a single soldier. On the back seats and the tailboard were piles of blankets, some clothes and a wooden box containing boots and tools. I could see from Miettinen's face that something was in the wind. After escorting the loggers to their work, the soldier in the jeep drove to town, parked outside Roosa and Luukas's house and personally carried all the gear into the hallway; he lit a cigarette and exhaled a few refreshing lungfuls of smoke before closing the front door and driving off again.

Not a word was said. But from that day on we lived under the same roof again, that boundless magnet had brought us together once more, things were as they should be, and it was eerie, as if we had done everything right yet still hadn't advanced – but we were relieved and happy, we were as free as you can be in a cage. The first night we were woken by a guard who wanted to make sure that no one had escaped; the night after that we weren't woken at all, merely inspected and counted, and on the third morning there weren't even tracks in the snow outside, we were getting to the end of January, it wasn't much more than six or seven degrees below zero, there was no wind, the sky was clouding over, and it was starting to snow again, hard, then the weather cleared and it became colder than ever.

But it didn't matter.

We were cutting wood. We were born to cut wood. I have never seen logging like it. Even Heikki had to shake his head and smile his toothless grin. The loggers were working as they would have done for the Russians, for their own, without arguing, and without breaking down, we skied, chopped wood, ate, slept and skied, plans develop from this, courage, thoughts about what might be possible, you become light headed, and one day it suddenly seems as if nothing awful can happen any more, as if everything is pure and clear, it is a dangerous thought, but by then we were already well into February.

Now reports from the front were changing tone one morning Miettinen came rushing into our kitchen and stood watching us as we ate breakfast before angrily announcing that we could stay inside today and rest, an order he strongly disliked, it was Sunday and Suomussalmi had never had so much wood, ha ha.

'Bastards,' he said.

Everything is like something, though you don't come to this conclusion until you think you have found a solution to something and it only turns out to be a repeat of something you thought before. And the period of waiting we were in now was like the time around Christmas when we were driven into the white hell. The only difference was that Suomussalmi was no longer going to fall, the town was not surrounded by solid enemy lines, and sooner or later we would have both milder days and night frosts, leaving an icy crust on the ground, on which skis do not leave tracks.

'I think the war will soon be over,' I said one evening to Antonov, whose eyes in recent days had displayed the same restlessness they had before we lost everything. He looked at me and agreed, the war was over, we would soon be surplus to requirements, but we had already been practising the next part of the plan.

We jumped up and told the others, no voting this time, skis, food, clothes, poles . . . in a matter of minutes we were outside beneath the starry sky, on our way north, floundering white crows across crunching ice, the swish of ski poles and white breath, the brothers moving like lissom cats, Mikael chuckling, humming and shrieking, Antonov dogged and bent over the ski poles whose spikes we had sawn off, Suslov driven by an odd madness that lit up the massive beard he had grown; only Heikki seemed to take the whole thing as an everyday occurrence, or a path leading home.

Everything that had been gathering during this eternity, ocean upon ocean of impenetrable darkness, drove us north in a focused march no one could stop, towards my farmstead north of Lonkkaniemi, the goal that, at the beginning of January, had seemed more unattainable than heaven; now we were doing it in one long, silent, arduous operation.

When we arrived in the early hours of the morning and could stand on the ice in front of the dark buildings and confirm that everything was in order – no tracks and nothing destroyed – without a word or any hesitation we got down to doing what had to be done, as if we had already survived, skis inside, dry wood, no light, only heat, bake bread, tins and salted meat, coffee, fruit jam, spirits, beds and shifts, the brothers fell asleep in each other's arms in my parents' bed, the rest of us sat and drank spirits and tentatively peered around in the daylight that slowly began to fill the undisturbed rooms, and listened to a question we still didn't have the strength to answer, but which would engulf us with a vengeance in the coming days. What now? – but not just yet. We had arrived, we had come as far as it was possible to go, for the time being, for men like us, who are worthless.

14

The next evening it became clear that the brothers had thought thoughts that were greater than both themselves and me: they wanted to continue north or west, preferably with me as their guide, towards Sweden or Norway, which were neutral countries. And in the course of the next few hours this idea also caught the imagination of Antonov, who previously had only wanted to get back home to his family in Kalevala.

But by that stage I, too, had had a little time to think, and from what I had heard in Suomussalmi, Sweden and Norway's betrayal of Finland didn't necessarily mean that they would take kindly to Russian deserters; quite the opposite – these countries feared the Soviet Union.

'We are not Russians,' Nadar said. 'We are Jews.'

Antonov threw up his hands with a chilling laugh. And again Nadar started to scream. We were back in a doomed siege mentality.

'He says that at home it makes no difference,' Antonov translated in a voice of despair. 'We'd be killed there, Jews and Russians alike. But that's . . .'

He suddenly changed tactics and screamed back: 'Have you got a passport, you coward? Do you go around with a passport that says you're a Jew?'

While he translated, Nadar stood looking down at his socks and mumbling something which twice I had to ask the peasant to explain, and as he did so he seemed drained.

'He says they have only got this one chance. And now he wants to know which is worse, Norway or Sweden. He also says that if you don't want to come with us, they'll try to make it on their own, they can manage, and they also want to know if you've got a map.'

I looked at the stocky peasant.

'It's a long way.'

'Nothing is a long way, not any more, not for them.'

'And are you going with them?'

He bided his time.

'I don't know, we may not be well received at home, but I've got a family and can't live anywhere else, and anyway, neither of them is . . .'

'Better to die at home than live in a foreign country?'

He smiled and said in his best Finnish:

'The snag with your question, angel, is you don't *know* if we'll be shot when we get home, nor whether we'll be allowed to live in Sweden. You said so yourself, we don't know *anything*, and the man who knows nothing goes home. Yes, I think that is probably what I shall do. Heikki has said he'll come with me as far as the border, and I'll find my own way home from there.'

He turned to look at Heikki. I did, too. The old man gave a self-conscious nod, he had his farm on the outskirts of Pirttivaara, close to the border, and all along he had been determined to return; even though he had no family there any more, he had land.

This conversation went on for several nights, back and forth, mulling over and putting into words all we needed to know to tell ourselves that once again we were trapped, blindly groping for another eye in a needle.

Suslov and Mikael didn't say a word. The teacher was bent forward in the solitary armchair, pulling at his beard, weighing up one factor against another, unable to make it all balance, he shook his head and snorted, got to his feet and then slumped back down, while Mikael sat in my father's rocking chair, sleepily staring out through the window that was now free of its ice flowers – it was sunny outside, spring-like and dazzlingly bright, we could hear the eaves dripping and creaks and groans in the timber walls, the freezing weather was relinquishing its grip – we had even heard swans.

'What about you, Mikael?' I shouted in Russian. 'What are you going to do?'

'I want to stay here,' he said.

The others smiled. 'We should have brought the cat,' he added, and carried on rocking. I stood up and said:

'Now let's rest and sleep. Tonight we'll bake more bread, we'll eat and drink, fire up the sauna and wash. We have clothes to wash, too.'

'Yes, yes, yes!' Suslov shouted, jumping up like an idiot and starting to dance around in a manner that caused the rest of us to look away in embarrassment.

We slept during the day, had the fire going only at night, never put on any lights, tiptoed around on the crusty snow in our stockinged feet, and the brothers quietly hummed over the pots and pans in the kitchen, unshakeable in their resolve to conquer a new world, though making the start was their problem. Mikael and I made a bed, placed an old straw mattress in it and put it in the attic, which was unused as I didn't have any brothers or sisters. Heikki and Antonov set traps for hares and wood grouse, while Suslov thought about whatever it was he was thinking about, tight lipped, thought and thought some more about something that was clearly beginning to tower up in front of him, like a mountain.

I both saw it and didn't see it. For the first time a new sense of unease had stirred in me, one I had never had a chance to feel in the town, we should have brought the cat with us, we should have cleaned Roosa and Luukas's house before we left, I should never have given the clock back to the man who owned it, remorse, I felt remorse, and realised that what I had done in Suomussalmi would obviously be regarded as treachery, the wood cutting and the intelligence reports, the things I had told the Russians about the surrounding country and farms and the conditions of the ice, I had tried to trick them, but there were no witnesses, and my ruses had not achieved anything anyway – my strongest card was the loggers, my sole and blessed witnesses, but they were Russians, the enemy, who I was now about to help leave the country, after that, not even God would be able to vouch for me.

So my story, like the loggers', didn't add up, and I couldn't bring myself to drive them away, to put an end to it all, or do something that would reveal our whereabouts, let alone join them, either to the north or the west, to leave Lonkkaniemi and Kiantajärvi for good. That was no more an option now than it had been when they were about to torch the town, I was who I was, in white wool, snow-blind, so I began to avoid the eternal discussions, went to bed and slept, at night, too.

Suslov occasionally came to my bedside and talked about something I didn't understand, but judging by what I could see of his glowing face it must have been something to do with his childhood, memories of something he was in the process of realising he could not return to, they weren't nice stories like the one about the boy and the horse, which had a meaning, they were fragments that just had to come out, like waste.

Mikael came as well, bringing weak coffee and a few small, hard water biscuits the brothers had baked. He didn't say anything, just sat staring out of the window with his hands resting on his knees like large, withered petals; we had everything where we were, just not the things we needed. But he was at peace, and it struck me that the worst the war had done to him was to age him, he had grown up, become a man, whatever good that might do him.

When the silence became too oppressive, I told him that in times past hens used to wander about in the snow, right beneath the window, they blackened the snow with their shit, so spring came first where they wanted it, the brown grass the herald of a new summer, and it would be like that again one day, I would get my horse Kävi back, I would buy a pig, or maybe a calf, eventually I would also get a new boat, there was a boat-builder in Suomussalmi I used to deliver wood to who would certainly let me have credit . . . At any rate he understood that this is the sort of thing you talk about, to get it out of your system.

We stayed put. Until Heikki announced one afternoon that the time had come, and that he would be leaving that night, before the snow deteriorated, a decision that knocked Antonov off kilter. He began to drag things out again, to get irritable, there was no rush, he was going home, yes, but not now, he had been thinking, yes, but hadn't finally decided yet . . .

I asked him what he was going to do, but he indulged himself in a contemptuous glance at Nadar, pulled me outside and asked again if it was a long way north, but interrupted himself before I could answer.

'They don't want me to go with them,' he said, resigned. 'They don't trust me.'

'Do you want to go with them?'

'They are Jews. I am a Russian.'

'Yes,' I said.

'So I would rather go home,' he said, 'with Mikael and the teacher.'

'Yes,' I said.

'Do you want to be rid of us?' he asked.

'No,' I said, looking him straight in the eye.

'Quite sure?'

'Yes. But if you stay, you'll be arrested sooner or later and sent home anyway.'

'What is best?'

'I don't know.'

He chewed his lips, and we stood looking at the forest, which was coated in rime and looked like an unbroken barbed-wire fence. We heard no sounds. We looked at each other, nodded as if we had just agreed on something, and went inside again. The brothers didn't look at us. Neither did Mikael in the rocking chair, his eyes closed, nor Suslov, immersed in his beard as usual.

Antonov whispered a few words to Heikki and took his hand. And Heikki said for all to hear that it made no difference to him, he could go alone, it was his country.

We loaded the small sled with food and equipment, gave him the best boots and skis, and said our goodbyes. And that night we stopped talking altogether, as if bound in a common understanding that if a single word passed between us, we would all perish – the brothers cooked dinner in silence, we ate in silence, Antonov and I chopped wood, and Mikael and Suslov waited for another starry spring night to pale into day. When I lay down to sleep, it was with a feeling of having lost one more little piece of the world, yet again, this time it was Heikki who had taken it with him, and I realised when we woke, some time in the afternoon, that only work could keep us going now, just as in Suomussalmi – we had better go over to the barn, I said, and get some axes and fishing nets, I had ten or so mooring ropes on the wooded headland, frozen solid in ice, but they could be cut free and used as sink-lines, that was the way we fished in the winter.

We set to work, put out four nets and returned to the house having seen neither man nor beast, hauled in the nets in the early hours of the morning, carried back the meagre catch and cooked it. We whiled away three nights doing this, putting out and hauling in nets, cooking the fish and eating it, I wanted to ask the brothers about this and that, but didn't. We chopped wood, even though it wasn't necessary, still spoke very little, washed frequently, and when Suslov came charging down from the attic on the fourth night and yelled that a skier was heading for the house, heading straight for the house!, I knew even before I saw the dangling ear-flaps that it was Heikki coming back, our friend Heikki.

He was sweaty, agitated and in a black mood. His farm had been burnt to the ground and the war was over; Finland had lost, not at Suomussalmi maybe, but on all the other fronts, and had had to hand over the territories the Russians demanded.

'I've got nowhere to go,' he said after confirming what we had all been waiting for, peace of a kind, a peace that perhaps could help us to get on with our lives. 'Can I stay here?'

Yes, we were where we were. In Lonkkaniemi. And that night another fight broke out between the brothers and Antonov, sparked off again by his wanting to go with them. Mikael sat in the rocking chair with his composed smile, as usual, and Suslov sat, stooped even farther into himself.

Heikki managed to calm them down, I couldn't, there were lots of things I couldn't manage these days that I would have done at any other time, but not now – I couldn't do anything. And then we turned in. But before I let myself slip back into those repugnant dreams, I knew that something now *had* to happen – in fact, that something *already had happened*.

I got up and saw the tracks from the window, deep, winding tracks from the house to the barn, the only ones made since we arrived.

Slowly I put on my clothes, woke Antonov and asked him to come with me. In the barn we found Suslov hanging from a hawser, his white face blue. He had cut off his beard and laid it like a furry animal next to the bench, which was lying on its side on the floor. There was also a sealed letter. We cut him down and Antonov let out a deep sigh. It was a turning point.

We woke the others. Although it was daylight, we carried Suslov to the headland. There we dug our way down to the forest floor and lit a large bonfire, let it burn for most of the day, then began to dig. Mikael had made a cross, he wept openly now, but his face didn't seem distorted, just lonely, and he insisted that I say something.

There was nothing to say. So I stood there and said it had been a long time since Suslov had told us the story about the boy who stole a horse and received a reward instead of punishment, and as I was saying this, with Antonov translating, his eyes closed, hands folded, as though reciting, it occurred to me that I could go on to mention that, in a way, we had lived in the same topsy-turvy world for as long as we had known each other, a world where right and wrong and up and down had exchanged places, and that even though we might have allowed ourselves to become confused, now we had to be clear headed again, we had realised, I said, without quite knowing what I meant, that we had become friends and that being friends was a crime, for all of us – it was Suslov who had given us this insight, through that terrible act of his, we thanked him, thought of him, and would never forget him.

The rest took its silent, muted course, for it really was over. The brothers decided to leave the following night, equipped with the sled, woollen blankets and a tarpaulin that could be used as a tent. The snow crust would hold for another week, maybe two, then they would have to find another way to travel. Antonov had, for his part, given up his plan of going with them, he wanted to go home, nothing else made any sense. And Mikael wanted to go with him.

I tore my father's old map in two, gave the brothers one half and Antonov the other. Food and equipment were also shared out amicably. Then we took our leave, promised to go to each other's funerals, gave fleeting smiles, shook each other's hands and all felt that things were happening too fast.

This time it was Antonov who had to say something, first in Russian, then in Finnish — he said something about courage, about *my* courage, but I immediately said no, I didn't want to hear any of that, it could equally well have been cowardice driving me, of course I knew what it took to survive, and survival was what I had wanted, I was afraid to die, scared to death, yes, put like that, a coward in a way.

Antonov smiled, but then he began to talk about strength, said that if I didn't have courage then I certainly had strength, the strength to do what had to be done, and I said no again — clearer now about my thoughts — said that I had drawn all the strength I had from the loggers' weakness, from the fact that, from the very beginning, their abject condition had revolted me, if they had been stronger than me, then I would have lost heart and become weak, like Suslov — that is what I said — and it is an advantage to be strong among those weaker, then you stay strong, and furthermore you can make others strong, too, that is what must have happened, at any rate I could never have managed it alone, and in a way — I realised that now — it was *they* who had saved me, just as much as I had saved them, and I wanted to thank them for that.

I don't know how Antonov translated this, but he made a conscientious attempt, the others nodded solemnly, and when he had finished I saw their bashful smiles, so I thanked them again, both in Finnish and Russian, before once more we shook hands and all left Lonkkaniemi.

Two men headed east towards the Soviet border, home, and two limping Jews went north-west, towards Norway or Sweden or wherever their hopes and strength might take them. And Heikki and I went south towards the immortal town of Suomussalmi, on the ice and clearly visible to the whole world now, and along the way I kept thinking how glad I was that I had thanked them — where had I got the idea from? I had got it from Suslov. And it was worth its weight in gold.

15

When the loggers Timo Vatanen and Heikki Turunen came to Suomussalmi one milky-white afternoon at the end of March 1940, the town had already made its first attempts to rise from the ashes. The civilian population was returning in impatient droves, new posts and white boards were erected over soot-blackened plinths, the blows of hammers rang out and circular saws were whining in the devastated forests, horses and trucks and tractors were loaded with the owners' most precious possessions, children playing in black slush, soldiers were without weapons, and civilians with tentative smiles on closed faces were milling around in a Bedouin-like camp of dirty army tents with crooked stovepipes spewing out smoke and pointing to a sky that from now on would only become milder and warmer as each day, each week passed, marking the road to spring and summer and new life in new houses.

That same night a party was thrown to the accompaniment of accordion music, tango and a drunken racket in the largest mess tent, erected in the school grounds, and that is one of the reasons why Timo refuses to say any more, for a terrible shame has overtaken him, shame over the fact that, despite restraining himself for a whole winter of war, in peacetime he found it necessary to hit the hard stuff and cut the guy ropes of the party tent, tear the canvas and start a fight with the now returned blacksmith, before being overpowered by three soldiers and locked up in a small workman's shed on wheels. It contained nothing but a stove the size of a tin can, two benches and a narrow table top, which Timo smashed to pieces with his bare fists to keep the fire going through the cold night, which, to the amusement and amazement of local people, he also spent banging on the walls and roaring:

'We're Russians! We're all Russians!'

It was Heikki who, after visiting family in Hulkonniemi, discovered in the early hours of the morning what had happened to his friend and went to release him. By then the town had settled down for the night.

'They'll be fine,' Heikki said, about the loggers. 'They'll be fine.'

'Yes,' said Timo.

Heikki went back to his relatives, and Timo made his way to Antti's house to sleep off the alcohol in his old back room.

Here the fury dissipated, but not the shame. He woke up, but did not go out, nor did he try to find food, and for the next few days he just sat at the window breathing on the glass and drawing letters in the condensation as sledges and cars passed by loaded up with wood and chattels and an increasing number of civilians returning to their burnt-out homes.

He kept this up until Antti and his sons also returned, excited and grateful to find their house intact and a skinny, distraught Timo, who sat guarding the shop as if he had done nothing else since they parted a whole eternity ago.

Timo helped them carry inside everything they had carried out at the beginning of December – three sled-loads of furniture and equipment and photos and clothes and boxes, the sewing machine and Anna's spinning wheel, which no one had any use for any more, but which was even more difficult to get rid of after the war, and a stock of tinned food and ten sacks of flour that the shopkeeper had been far sighted enough to pack on the smallest sled, pulled by Timo's horse, Kävi – the horse recognised its master, laid a drooling muzzle over his shoulder, a kind of hug, and Timo stroked his neck and flanks and noticed that it must have been in a stable for the winter, it was so well looked after and plump.

The shop reopened the following day, with an embarrassed Timo behind the counter, Antti and his sons having gone west again to fetch more goods – there was a desperate need for tools, timber, nails, tinned food, meat, coffee, flour . . . the only thing the town was well supplied with was wood. And it was only when Antti came back for the second time that Timo told him about his behaviour at the peace celebrations, and announced that he could not stay any longer, he wanted to go home to Lonkkaniemi, with Heikki, who had overstayed his welcome with relatives and was ready to start rebuilding his farm near the eastern border. Timo might help him with this, he did not know, he just knew he could not stay any longer in Suomussalmi, his own town, which not even a Russian army had managed to drive him out of. Now his shame had achieved that, an invisible black plague, but he wanted to ask Antti a favour first, a kind of return favour for having looked after his house: to be allowed to have the heap of scrap metal rusting in the spring sun outside Luukas and Roosa's house transported to Lonkkaniemi.

'Scrap metal?'

Yes, Timo had plans to transform it, if not into gold, then at least into usable tools he could sell perhaps, or find a use for himself among all the things that needed to be repaired and maintained on a farm like his – it was big, and he had no plans for it to become smaller.

Antti had observed that the war had not been kind to his friend. The young man had aged, there was a hollow in his face, as frightening as a hole in the ice, and he was obviously ill at ease in this time of peace when everyone else was jumping about with happiness, at least those who had not lost everything, family, home, everything. So Antti said no more about the scrap metal, just nodded that it would be done, as soon as the snow melted and the log trails were dried out; he could take Kävi with him at the same time.

'But don't stay away too long,' the shopkeeper added earnestly.

Timo promised not to stay away.

That night he and Heikki travelled north again, once more on the ice, and spent a few days in Lonkkaniemi. Timo then joined his friend on his journey east to help him erect the structure for a new farmhouse.

They finished in the early part of summer. Then they set to work putting on the roof and the weatherboarding. But how long must a silence last before you can decide whether it is good or bad?

'The borders are shut now,' Heikki said. 'We won't hear a word from them, not now, not later, perhaps ever.'

'No,' Timo said.

'But it doesn't mean anything. They're all right.'

'Yes,' Timo said.

'They were strong, remember that, they'd never been stronger than when they left.'

From then on, Timo was at home and did what he had always done, a bit of seasonal work — he had only a few fodder fields to keep in order, ditches to clean, timber, fishing, when he was not in his workshop repairing tools. Then the woodcutting time came around again and he made his days long and strenuous so that he did not have to lie awake during the light nights with all those thoughts screaming in the silence. He waited for them to fall quiet, waited for his shame to fade away, to be brought to an end, and perhaps especially for the memory of the Russian loggers to disappear. He saw them as they fell asleep, one after the other, next to the burning boat shed. Even Antonov had been forced to fold his stiff hands. A human life is not worth much, but still you cling to it when you have it, and often in a sentimental way, and this sentimentality too had left a deep imprint on Timo's mind — these poor miserable creatures whom, on an impulse from an inaudible voice, he had saved and perhaps in so doing himself too, only to become once more — under such dramatic circumstances as a war — a wanderer in his own existence; it was no use shaking his shoulders, it would not go away, nor could he sweep it aside as if he were swatting flies or mosquitoes, these buzzing, steaming summer swarms that encircled his sweaty body from morning to night and which he only escaped when he was indoors or when he immersed himself in the waters of Lake Kiantajärvi, and then swam with such lazy strokes that he floated, out into the bright, windless evenings there were so many of that summer, this pure reward, this light.

Even though more than five thousand bodies had been recovered from the ice in the winter and spring, the lake had swallowed many more, and these lay rotting in the deep and in the bays. Timo had found several just by following fox tracks and flocks of crows. The black water was no longer clear, there were more wolves in the forests than ever, and there was always someone behind him, a snorting horse, a shadow outside the window as he looked up from a plate of roast pork, the water lilies and the rushes stroking his stomach and thighs as he glided like a white fish through all that had once been the way it should be, warm and cool and eternal – someone had been there, and had taken it away.

When August arrived, Timo decided to buy a pig – although it was late in the year, he needed a pig. And now he was heading south by boat. He rowed, it took time, and it bored him, and it did not usually, he liked to row, and now it was a golden, mellow day in late summer with forest and sky on all sides, the boat making oil-smooth ripples on the vast mirror-like surface. He rowed faster and felt the sweat and the blood and the wet wood of oars and rowlocks rubbing gently against the silence, it is something that never ends, but it *has* to end.

Then he saw the town, a half-finished town of pale wood, a town on its knees, for the present, a town on its way up, bowed and so beautiful, and shining peerlessly in the evening sun as never before, and he had to step on to the shore and stand staring, gaping like the ungainly wreck that he was – he could have opened and read the letter Suslov had left behind, but he had not, he knew what was in it, the same as in the note the teacher had left in Roosa's glasses case when they fled for the first time, it said thank you and nothing else, there was nothing else it could say.

He moored the boat and walked with resolute steps up to the blacksmith he had attacked during the peace celebrations and said that he had come to apologise and, in addition, to order some new metal fittings for a wood-cart; he described in detail what they should look like, the measurements, the thickness and shape of the iron, the bolt holes . . . the blacksmith took notes and they shook hands after settling on far too high a price and agreeing on a collection date of just under a week.

He intended to go to see Antti, but now that he was there, he stopped outside Luukas and Roosa's house and stood admiring the new porch, as well as the freshly painted kitchen and sitting-room windows, then he knocked and went into the hall and on into the kitchen, to the old couple who were sitting there and who had lost their son, Markku, on the isthmus, but they still had two sons alive, who had also been soldiers, and he asked in a low voice if they had seen a grey cat, a cat with no tail.

They had not.

Timo felt the distance that had grown between them, for although they greeted him and gave him coffee and Roosa told him about Markku, Luukas said less than usual, did not make any jokes or ask any questions. So Timo remained sitting attentively, his head hanging, after the coffee had been drunk and the cakes eaten. Until Luukas stood up with a sigh, produced a small notepad he kept in the drawer where Timo had found the glasses, and a pencil, sat down next to him and placed a hand on his shoulder.

'Look at me, Timo, when I'm speaking to you.'

Timo looked at him. Luukas said:

'We'll do what we usually do. I want three loads in October, thirty centimetres, birch, not dry spruce, not pine, birch!'

He slowly wrote down the order and gave Timo the piece of paper. Timo looked at it with tears in his eyes, folded it, put it in his shirt pocket and hurried out.

'I'll be here! In October! I'll be here!'

*

He wondered whether he should also pay a visit to the man with the marsh-brown beard, to demand what he was owed, but instead he went straight to see Antti. There he found the shop and the front door locked. But the back door was open, as usual, Timo's door, to his own room, so he went inside and got in between freshly laundered sheets and fell asleep before the silence descended over the town, and now he saw neither the stony faces of shame nor those of the Russians, only forest, which might be cut down one day or else allowed to live, immense tracts of forest.

After waking he made himself a hearty breakfast, ticked off the number of meals taken by Timo Vatanen on the piece of paper above the worktop, and also wrote a short message for Antti. But on his way to the farmer who was to sell him the piglet, he bumped into Olli, the lieutenant who was still a lieutenant, though now wearing civilian clothes.

But the eternal lieutenant walked quickly past him and looked away – he had more important things on his mind than recognising a man he, strictly speaking, had received orders to evacuate from the town last winter. And Timo was taken aback by this, as he would gladly have stood before Olli, even with bowed head. But now he felt stronger too, almost normal, so instead he went to see the man with the marsh-brown beard and stood by as he hesitated before paying up, fumbled with his money, counted it twice, then a third time, before handing it over with an expression that suggested he had been the victim of a despicable swindle.

'Thank you,' Timo said. 'I know you don't like to be in debt.'

'Thank *you*,' the man said.

Then he went to buy the piglet, bargained its price down as low as he could, carried it to the boat, tethered it in the stern and rowed home again on a mirror that was even smoother than it had been the day before. He did not want to read Suslov's letter this time either. He knew what was in it, and besides, he could not read Russian.

16

Timo's first autumn was spent doing the things that have to be done – making hay and drying grass for Kävi's winter fodder, fishing, picking berries, hunting and cutting wood. He delivered his orders at the appointed time, birch, dry spruce, pine, people's tastes vary. The newly built shell of the school had been fitted with stoves that swallowed metre-long timbers, while old Babushka wanted tiny log-ends, chippings almost, for her tiled stove, and the payment was as it had always been, it was low, or else Timo was paid in kind, usually food, so when the frozen-hard October fields, so pleasant underfoot, were covered with November snow, he had everything he needed to hunker down for another new winter – security, peace, plans.

So it went on. For him. There was a new war. The Continuation war even more destructive than the first. But it was not his War. Timo was at home, supplying wood to those who needed it, to the embattled regiments as well when they were in the area and taking in frozen soldiers and lighting the fire in the sauna and giving them what food he had. Heikki stayed with him for a while, too, since once again it was impossible for him to live at home, in his reconstructed farmhouse – they did the same things together, hunting, fishing and cutting wood. Heikki drank heavily all the time, Timo did not drink at all.

When this new war was over, and it turned out that Heikki's farm had been razed to the ground for a second time, they went east and rebuilt it. Heikki was well over sixty, but he had to have a place to live, a farm to run, land to own, land to cultivate, a home, the one where he was born and where it was his firm intention to die. But he had no furniture.

Timo gave him the bed he and Mikael had made, two kitchen chairs and a small stove. Then they made two tables, benches and cupboards for the new kitchen, cupboards for the hallway, too. In addition, they got some old junk from Antti and Roosa, a worn couch, a chest of drawers, an armchair the size of a moose, and, bit by bit, all the cutlery and pots and pans an unmarried man who only very seldom had any other company could need.

*

And now the peace was real. It was total. But it was also inert, lonely and wretched, not that Timo particularly noticed, except that his loads of wood still had to be paid for with more food than he could manage to eat. So he gave the surplus to Heikki, who struggled for a few years before getting back on his feet again, or to an orphanage in Peranka, for which he also supplied wood without any payment, he had visited the place himself and offered his services free of charge on the pretext that he himself had grown up in an orphanage, it was Mikael who had put this idea into his head. That was how he thought of the Russian loggers now, they had given him ideas, he could look upon them in the same way that he looked upon his mother and father, as faces on a transparent wall, people it was appropriate to recognise and remember, nothing was missing, it was over and you could do nothing about it, they were Russians, behind a border that not even a word could slip through.

But even though the next decades passed quietly for both Timo and his Suomussalmi, something dramatic happened to the town's standing, to its name and reputation. History took over, History with a capital H. Those things that would be selected from the swirling confusion of the past, to be written down and remembered, had finally been separated from the chaff that would be discarded and forgotten. And from this vast stocktaking the tiny, burnt-out town in the most desolate of all forests suddenly appeared in the curricula of the world's leading military academies – motti tactics at their brilliant best could be studied in Suomussalmi's beautiful surroundings, where a modern, fifty-thousand-strong Russian army had found itself locked in a vice-like grip of freezing temperatures and iron, and was cut to pieces and brought to its knees by a few white-clad troops on skis, without artillery, tanks or any air support. That is how war should be waged, defensive warfare at its most glorious.

Well-dressed delegations arrived in Suomussalmi, Finnish and foreign, veterans and civilians, politicians and academics; the President made an appearance in the new town hall and was presented with a huge bouquet of flowers and a memento of the war, a thermos flask that had saved the life of Captain Lassila, perhaps the greatest of all heroes; the war museum in Raatevaara was founded and became a worthy, low-profile testimony to the minor nation's great achievement. And it happened fast, from one day to the next, it was suddenly there, as if people had always known, but only now had understood, accepted and come to terms with it. The sun was shining on Suomussalmi once more, this time 'for all eternity', as the President expressed it.

But most of the pomp and ceremony passed Timo by like a quiet summer's day. He worked, he read newspapers and listened to the radio when he was with Antti, registered that once again he had become an unsung ballad in someone else's epic, a magician without a hat, as it should be. He chopped the wood he had to and earned money, enough to be able to buy an old tractor when Kävi died, and then a tiny little egg-shaped caravan, too, which he bought as scrap, it was to stand in Antti's new storeroom for many years waiting for a car. But eventually there was a car, an American car, which Timo clambered underneath and fiddled with whenever he was in Suomussalmi. One day, perhaps, it would tow his caravan to faraway places, to Inari, Rovaniemi or Oulu, if he felt so inclined.

But then he was given an article written by an American, translated into Finnish and printed in a newspaper in Kajaani, a long and detailed article about the Winter War, Timo's war. And in it the writer talked about Rodion and the ladies' shoes, although he did not mention the name, but it was written down in black and white that a Russian soldier had been taken prisoner near Suomussalmi in January 1940, a man the Finnish troops had taken to – because of those shoes he refused to relinquish – and kept during the final stages of the war as a sort of helper or mascot. Later he had been granted amnesty and remained in Finland, in Joensuu apparently, with his Finnish family.

There was no photograph of him, and he did not play

any further part in the article, which, as usual, was about the heroes who had fought and died on the road between Suomussalmi and Raatevaara, what became known as the Road of Death.

But it was a drop. In fact it was the first drop of rain on the last day of a welcome dry spell for haymaking. And Timo began to wonder. It did not bother him that he was not mentioned in the article, as Rodion's saviour, for instance. But it did seem strange, the more he thought about it, that the Russian – after so many years in Finland! – had never made any attempt to trace him, the distance between Joensuu and Suomussalmi was not insurmountable, there was no border between them, just woodland and many different roads, unless of course Rodion had been held back by something else, by an external force, or an internal one, shame, or some unknown Russian emotion the workings of which no one could understand.

While Timo was lying under the Ford that autumn, which was to prove so different from all the others he had lived through since the war, another raindrop fell, a new article based on the findings of a Norwegian historian who had discovered that two Russian Jews – brothers – had managed to cross the border to Finnmark in the wake of the Winter War, and from there had made their way south along the Norwegian coast, by boat, all the way to Trondheim, where they had been taken care of by a family who made their living selling coal and groceries. But then war had broken out in Norway, too, and the whole family, including the Russian brothers, had been betrayed, arrested by the German occupying forces and sent by ship to Poland to be burnt in ovens.

You could say the heavens opened.

It was twenty years since Timo had watched Leo and Nadar limp north on the snow crust, two contorted figures on a clear spring night, setting out on their impossible journey towards a new life. And now he began to behave like everyone else in the district, scouring newspapers and books for everything that had been written about Suomussalmi during all his quiet years, there was a huge amount – the town had been a little Stalingrad on Finnish soil for the Russians – and only a couple of weeks after he had read the article by the Norwegian professor, he came across a story about Antonov and Mikael. According to a national newspaper, a Russian defector had informed Western embassy staff in Helsinki that about a hundred fugitives had been taken prisoner and shot as deserters as soon as they had crossed the border after the collapse in the north. The defector was able to name over thirty of the victims, among them an Antonov – but no Mikael! – and in response to questions about how he came to be so well informed, he had reluctantly admitted his past as an officer in the Red Army, which presumably made him an accessory to the massacre, but it also made him a credible eyewitness, not least because he was also able to provide details about the fate of Oleg Illyushin, the Russians' commanding officer in Suomussalmi. The colonel had also managed to return safely to his native country, only to be sentenced to death by a summary court and shot, together with three other officers – 'for having let the enemy capture fifty-five field kitchens'.

Timo spent days on all the things that were coming to his attention now. It was like a conspiracy, some of it made no sense. He discussed it with Antti, who was now confined to a wheelchair, and had handed over the shop and firewood business to his eldest son, Harri; Antti always had a shifty look in his eyes when Timo talked to him about his Winter War, the winter that, of all Finns, he *alone* had experienced in all its phases – as he never tired of pointing out.

'It's as if none of it ever happened,' Timo said.

'What do you mean?'

'As my father used to say, when it's all in vain, it might just as well not have happened.'

Timo tried to smile. He stood there with an unread letter and no witnesses, and forced a smile. It was so long ago, and yet it was yesterday. But Antti just said what he always said, Timo should not worry about it, the world was and always would be incomprehensible and unreal and trying to fathom it out would not make it the slightest bit more intelligible.

'But what about his wife?' Timo insisted, Rodion's wife, for whom those shoes had been intended, how could he not go back to her after all the yearning and suffering he had gone through, even Antonov would not have got through without his family, a family is everything for those who have one, there was nothing Timo would rather have had than a family, although he did have Antti.

The shopkeeper could not answer that one. In fact, he did not know much at all about this story, which came as a surprise to Timo.

'He lives in Joensuu,' he said, as if that were an argument.

'I see,' Antti said.

'That's what it says here . . . !'

Timo also went to see his old teacher, Marja-Liisa Lampinen, who had grown so bitter after her beauty had retreated like a crushed army. She had long ago left teaching but worked part-time at the war museum in Raatevaara, and in her old age she was reputed to be the foremost expert in precisely what went on in this part of the country that famous winter.

But she was not interested in Rodion or the other loggers either. She quite simply doubted what Timo told her, said so to his face, even though he stood there waving his newspaper cuttings at her. Instead she began to talk in an impatient radio voice about his 'war traumas', as if it were the kind of fact you could find in her museum, she could not even be bothered to afford him the patience he could normally count on, and then she brought it all to a cruel conclusion:

'Nadar isn't a Jewish name.'

'What?'

'I think it might be Hungarian.'

'And Leo?'

'That may be Jewish, like Levi . . . but a Jewish family doesn't give *one* of the sons a Hungarian name and the other . . . and there's something wrong with the other names too, some are only surnames, Antonov and Suslov, and others are only first names. Whatever the reason, it's just nonsense, Timo! Do you understand, for example, what I'm saying now?'

She said a sentence in Russian.

'No.'

'As I thought. And I'll tell you another thing. These Russian defectors are not to be trusted, they'll say anything as long as it sounds credible, so as to be allowed to stay here.'

'One of those killed was called Antonov.'

She took the newspaper cutting from him, read it, then held it up with a triumphant smile of the kind he remembered all too well from the days when she was attractive and, in contrast to now, most things could be forgiven.

'It says here that this massacre took place east of the Kuhmo front, and that's quite a long way from here, Timo. Besides, Antonov is a very common name. It's just nonsense, Timo, can't you see, it's all just nonsense, and this interpreter, how did you ever think him up?'

Timo went home to Lonkkaniemi that night thinking that he had heard a mixture of good and bad news and it was impossible to disentangle one from the other, it seemed more like an exercise in confusion than ordinary silence, the silence that grows out of limits as well as time, which everyone could enjoy after a war, including himself, and then he began to wonder why the old cow had not gone on again about him chopping wood for the Russians, her, the woman who had never deprived herself of anything, he had cut wood for himself, to live!

Even though he could walk past the cross at Lonkkaniemi every day and see it standing there as proof, of Suslov, the man with only a surname, who had been buried with Roosa's glasses, that was the least they could do for him, let him keep the glasses – it became clearer and clearer to him that he had to do something unless he wanted to be haunted by shadows again, to gather evidence, as it were. Then he hit upon the perfect pretext for visiting Olli, the lieutenant who was still alive and living a few hours' drive away to the west, on the outskirts of Kajaani – Timo could simply knock on his door and demand his rifle back, the rifle he had not had a sniff of since it was confiscated, and it was not just a gun, it was a family heirloom his father had used to defend himself against the Reds during the civil war, when Finland fought against Finland and not against Russia. Did the eternal lieutenant have any idea at all of the range of that rifle, Timo's rifle?

Fired up by this idea, he wrote three letters, three very important letters, and went back to Suomussalmi to post them. Then he spent the next few days making the final adjustments to the Ford, and one Sunday in late November, slowly but surely, he drove off along the gravel roads towards the largest town he had ever seen and, with a little help, found where Olli lived, a square house on a square piece of land covered with short, evenly cropped grass.

But this expedition did not lead him any closer to what were becoming increasingly vague perceptions in his mind, either. Olli had grown old and had difficulty getting about, was bald and refused to let him in, even claimed he did not recognise him, then said, well, yes, maybe. His face fell, so they just stood there on the porch in the dank autumn weather.

'The war? The rifle?'

If it were true, enquiries would have to be made at the army depots, but it was a very long time ago, and he could not remember any rifle . . .

'But you remember *me!*'

'No, I don't . . .'

The lieutenant was contrariness itself. And it did not help matters that he looked as if he were scared he was going to be presented with an old bill. Timo's mind jammed and, waving his newspaper cuttings about again, he shouted:

'I'm absolutely convinced . . . I'm absolutely convinced that . . . *strange* things go on in every war.'

That was the word that came to him, *strange*. And the lieutenant was apparently none the wiser. He made a decent attempt at escaping, but Timo grabbed him, tried to focus attention on the loggers, the mysteries, as though trying to save them once again, to repeat the good deed, once was not enough, *and why doesn't anyone remember anything?* But before this mess could lead somewhere his mind shut down and he caught sight of the curious meadow surrounding the lieutenant's house.

'What's that over there?' he snapped, indicating a closely cropped meadow, not brown like any ordinary stubble field at this time of the year, but green and fresh, a dwarf meadow.

'Lawn,' Olli said.

'What?'

'It's called a lawn; it's common nowadays, you mow it once a week.'

Timo shrugged and gave a few hoarse grunts, called Olli an old fool and said he could keep the rifle and take it and his whole rotten life, and the lawn and go to hell.

He heard angry shouting behind him as he strode across the lawn, felt the softness beneath his rough boots, like moss, silk, down, newly fallen snow.

'Why *now?*' came a shout.

Timo had never heard anything so stupid, he gave him the cold shoulder again, got into the car and drove back, determined to find a person, a journalist or a student, someone who could write and tell his story one day, so that it could tower up like an immovable mountain face that would never crumble away, as he was witnessing now, a story without faltering or prevarication, a whole book – for everyone has the right to be a hero in his own life, even the lame and the blind, even those with a festering crater in their face, albeit with a little help. Where would we be without a little help? It seemed like an inspiring idea for an act of revenge, another idea the immortal Suslov had given him when he shouted at Antonov, *If you are not happy with the story, then bloody well write your own!*

This amused him. This was what he decided and rejected and decided anew as the heavy forest landscape on both sides of the fine, straight road was swallowed up by the gathering evening darkness, and a light rain began to fall, so that Timo got to try out his windscreen wipers, which worked, as did the lights. Even though, for safety's sake, he slowed down, only very rarely meeting any oncoming traffic, and arrived home in Suomussalmi well before midnight.

As usual, he found the back door unlocked, went inside, lay down and slept the way he had always done before reading about Rodion in the American article. What was in the newspapers was no truer than what slopped around like ditchwater in a poor wretch's memory, just more confusing, the Rodion in the paper did not even have a name, and Finland did not give amnesty or citizenship to Russian prisoners of war, no matter how many high-ranking officers begged and pleaded for them, it was as simple as that, it was all made up, the lot of it, and not even that old cow of a teacher realised.

17

Another winter passed, the twenty-sixth since Timo Vatanen had taken part in the war that was to fill his life to the brim with unsolvable mysteries and without a single answer to any of his letters. They were not even returned. It was quiet on both this and the other side of the border. So perhaps they were not that important. When he turned fifty-six at the end of March he ate a cake that Antti's son had ordered from a family baker in Hyrynsalmi. It came by bus.

They all sat in the sitting room of Antti's new home, which Timo had equipped with a ramp so that his friend could move his wheelchair in and out as he wanted.

It was not a big party, just Harri and Jussi with their wives, but they had a swarm of children who ran around having a whale of a time. After a while, alcohol also appeared on the table, and for once Timo did not say no.

'I hear you're planning to go away this summer,' Jussi said.

'Yes,' Timo said, suddenly quite calm. 'I might take the caravan, if I finish doing it up. To Joensuu.'

'Joensuu. What are you going to do there?'

'Well, I'm not sure. I've never been there, have you?'

'No. And I can't see any reason to go there, either.'

'Nor me,' Timo laughed.

Over the winter he had spent a lot of his savings on equipping the caravan: new tyres, mudflaps with reflectors, a water tank in one of the small cupboards above the bed; the axle was reinforced with two bars and a cable was run from the car to activate the rear lights.

But he had also rued some of these expenses because there was a lot that needed doing in Lonkkaniemi. He should have electricity put in, for example, and the road could be improved to make it more than a tractor lane, a road he could drive his caravan along even when it was not frozen.

Jona's youngest daughter was five years old. Her name was Tiina and she was the most beautiful child Timo had ever seen. Now she came and climbed up on his broad lap.

'Daddy has asked me to say,' she said with a little pause between each word and a shy smile, '. . . . because it's your birthday today . . . that without you we would all freeze.'

Timo smiled.

'You said that very nicely,' he said, touched. 'And it's absolutely true, too. Wait, I'll take a photo of you.'

He went to his caravan and got the camera, took a photo of Tiina, who had sat herself on the table, then one of everybody and afterwards got Harri and then Jona to take a photo of him, Timo, together with the others.

'Where did you get this?' Harri asked, referring to the camera.

'I bought it in Kajaani last year,' Timo said. 'These are the first pictures I've taken. Look here, number four.'

He stayed the night in Suomussalmi, spent most of the next day putting the finishing touches to the caravan, and did not drive the tractor north until very late that night, over the ice. All day he had sensed something in the air, and he had also thought about Heikki, who had said the same just before he died, that he had felt it and waited for it, for death, before the stroke hit him. And when he saw the farm in Lonkkaniemi that clear spring night, he felt it again. There was someone there.

He parked the tractor in its usual place, under the lean-to next to the barn, took a walk around the house, then went indoors and lit the fire. Then he went out again and watched the smoke rising towards the lustreless stars. The feeling would not let go. He went back in and started to look for

Suslov's letter. It was not where it usually was, on top of the cabinet in the sitting room, someone must have taken it, or he might have put it somewhere himself, he had become very forgetful lately, although it was many years since he had stood before a locked door and had been unable to find his name.

He went outside again, to the tip of the headland to look at Suslov's cross, a simple wooden cross which he had repaired several times. In the mornings it cast a shadow to the west, in the evenings to the east, and in the middle of the day a short shadow to the north, he could not quite work it out, anyway it looked like an oval sundial, an eye, if you saw it from above, and then suddenly he knew what it was, this low, deep sigh that had passed through the forest and the sky for the last day. The war was over, the night of 26 March 1967.